THE LAST APRIL

THE LAST APRIL

AN OHIO CIVIL WAR NOVEL

BELINDA KROLL

BRIGHT BIRD PRESS
Columbus, Ohio

This book is a work of historical reconstruction, and therefore a work of fiction.
The appearance or mention of certain historical figures is inevitable. Names,
characters, places, and incidents are the product of the author's imagination or are
used fictitiously. For the purpose of the story, the author condensed the timeline
of certain historical events. Any resemblance to actual events, locales, or persons,
living or dead, is coincidental or historically-inspired. The aftermath of Abraham
Lincoln's assassination, however, was very real.

Bright Bird Press
Columbus, Ohio 43221

ISBN (paperback): 978-0-9830786-5-4
eISBN: 978-0-9830786-6-1
Library of Congress Control Number: 2016963563

First Edition
Edited by Second Set of Eyes
Produced by PressBooks

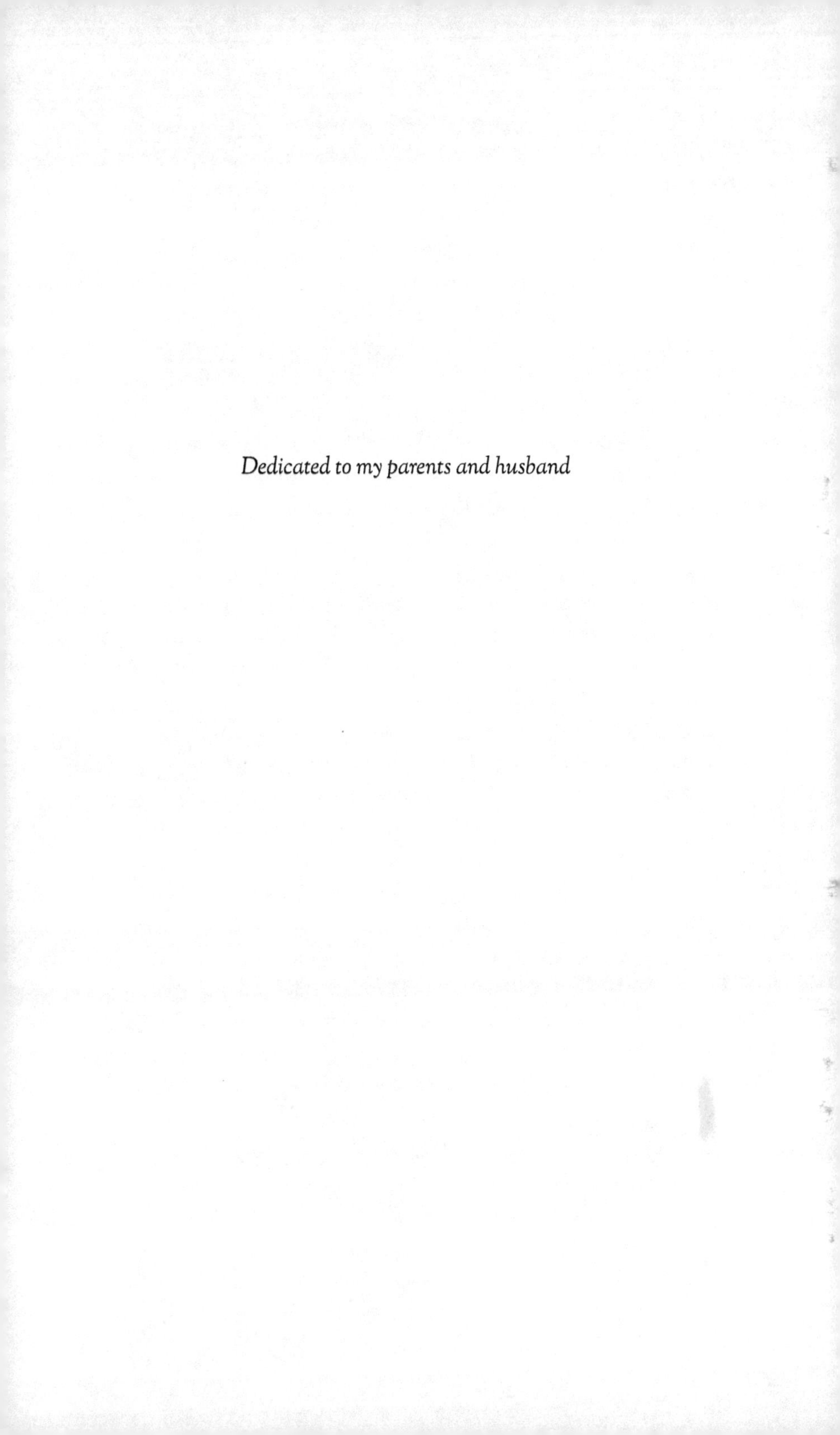

Dedicated to my parents and husband

ONE

Saturday, 15 April 1865 / Columbus, Ohio

Everyone else would remember that Saturday as the day President Lincoln died. Gretchen Miller would remember it as the day the ragged man collapsed at her feet.

Gretchen was tugging at weeds and swatting at gnats when a thud made her whip around. The war was over, but Confederate supporters were everywhere. They lingered after General Lee's surrender, and President Lincoln's reconciliation speech, and in pro-Union Columbus.

Gretchen swung from her hunched position to lean back on her barefoot heels. Her skirts puffed out with the movement. She slapped them down, annoyed.

Sharp sunlight made it difficult to see. Gretchen thought she saw a collapsed man just yards from her hem. She adjusted her straw hat so it shaded her eyes.

The man was sprawled across the oak tree roots. Gretchen could not tell his age or condition from where she crouched. His back was to her, his dark head resting on his outstretched arm. He was not moving.

"May the angels have charge of me," Gretchen whispered. She patted the revolver in her skirt pocket.

His leg twitched.

Gretchen's heart leaped. That dark, matted hair gave her a turn. Maybe it was her brother Werner, returned from war at last. A hundred men from the Grove City area had answered President Lincoln's call for soldiers. Everyone was afraid of the number that would return.

Gretchen grabbed her skirts as she scrambled to standing. She flailed her arms at the log farmhouse she called home. She could not shout, in case the man had faked his injury and was waiting for an excuse to attack.

Her aunt, Tante Klegg, stuck her head out the kitchen door. "What is it?" Tante Klegg's heavy German accent was strident in the quiet morning. It matched the severity of her hair braided and twisted tight against her head.

Gretchen put her finger to her lips. She cupped her hands around her mouth so her whisper would carry. "There is a man." She waved at her aunt to come outside.

Tante Klegg tiptoed across the rocks Gretchen had overturned gardening. She held her skirt layers high above her ankles.

The man remained quiet, only his twitching foot letting them know he lived. Gretchen did not know if that meant he was dangerous or that he was too injured to move.

Gretchen brushed a strand of reddish hair from her mouth as the breeze picked up. Though it was April, the humidity was heavy and stifling. The wind still carried the scent of cooling bonfires from yesterday's elaborate celebrations.

Last night, Gretchen had danced until her feet ached and sung until her voice was hoarse. She had been ready to do anything to help her country heal. She held onto the president's words of reconciliation that she read in the newspaper. She hoped everyone could see the Confederates as prodigal brothers and sisters. She hoped the Confederates would be humble and welcomed home.

With a stranger at her feet, Gretchen realized such things were easier said than done. She gripped the revolver hidden in her pocket and held out her other hand to stop her aunt from advancing. Holding her breath, she crept closer.

The man perhaps could have been her brother, once upon a time. His body was gaunt, worn thin by trials Gretchen suspected she would never understand. His left hand did not bear Werner's distinctive strawberry-shaped birthmark.

This was not her brother.

"So young," Gretchen said. Like Werner, the man could not have been more than two years older than she was.

Gretchen noted the hollows in his cheeks, which gave him a stark, haunted air even as he slept. His breath was shallow, but labored. His skeletal shoulder jerked under her light touch. He heaved a shuddering breath and turned dazed eyes on her.

The revolver in Gretchen's skirt pocket had the hammer pulled and the bullet loaded. She could yank the trigger and shoot a bullet through her skirts and into his chest, but the recoil would hurt. She would have to decide fast.

"Have I done it?" he said. His voice cracked and had a distinct drawl.

"Have you done what?" Gretchen said.

"Escaped."

The hairs on the back of Gretchen's neck stood on end. "Escaped? From where?"

"Camp Chase." He watched her a moment before his eyes rolled back.

A chill ran down Gretchen's back. Camp Chase was the training barracks four miles due west of Columbus. The government converted a part of it into a Confederate prison not too long after the war started.

Gretchen shook him. His eyes opened to slits.

"Water. Been walking two days." He lost consciousness.

He hardly looked well enough to have made the five-mile walk to her farm from Camp Chase. Her brother Werner had done it often in a day, but he had been healthy and energetic.

Gretchen frowned.

Tante Klegg approached. "He is not dead?" She sounded annoyed by the inconvenience.

Gretchen shook her head. She wondered how a dead man would have been any more convenient than a fainted one.

"What is it you plan to do?"

"What I plan to do?" Gretchen echoed. Somehow, because she had found the stranger, he was her responsibility. Gretchen might have felt peeved had the idea of solving a mystery not taken hold. "He looks like Werner, doesn't he?" she asked, her head cocked to the side.

Tante Klegg lifted her hands, signaling she did not care. "And?"

"And... I... think we need to move him in the shade. He is bleeding, and thirsty, and likely starved." Gretchen did not bother mentioning he had escaped from prison.

Tante Klegg grunted. "We will bring him inside." She rolled him over so they could grab his arms and legs.

Gretchen wondered if her brother was as starved as this man. She imagined Werner trying to get home and failing. She imagined Werner falling at the feet of a girl who wanted to do her part to bring the country back together.

Her father and brother had disappeared fighting for the Union's sovereignty. Gretchen would do her part, though she was just a farm girl from little Grove City, Ohio.

Gretchen hoped her father and brother had someone like her to help them. She hoped they were in a safe house, with someone who cared about bringing together North and South, Union and Confederate, abolitionist and slaveholder.

In the meantime, Gretchen needed to get this man out of sight.

PRESIDENT LINCOLN'S RECONSTRUCTION SPEECH

Tuesday, 11 April 1865 / The White House

We all agree that the seceded States, so called, are out of their proper particular relation with the Union, and that the sole object of the Government, civil and military, in regard to those States, is to again get them into that proper relation.

...Let us all join in doing acts necessary to restore the proper practical relations between these States and the Union, and each forever after innocently indulge in his own opinion whether in doing such acts he brought States from without into the Union...

TWO

____

Saturday, 15 April 1865 / Grove City, Ohio

He woke in the luxury of a straw tick bed. His bones ached in ways he had never dreamed possible. The beds at Camp Chase were little more than wooden slats. The hospital lacked the funds and inclination to make their prisoners comfortable.

Rather than hearing shuffling prisoners aiding bedridden peers, he heard... a bird, chirping, and the pleasant hum of insects he associated with a hot, humid day. Maybe everyone was asleep and that was why he could not hear the Camp Chase hustle.

But then there was the fact that the room did not smell right. It should have smelled like unwashed bodies or the stench of those dying and dead of cholera. Instead, there was a powdery sort of floral scent that reminded him of...

Well, something. He just could not think of what it was.

"Gretchen, he wakes," he heard a woman say.

He opened his eyes to see wide skirts sweeping from the room. That confirmed it. He was not at Camp Chase. The only woman allowed in the prison had died a year ago, of the smallpox she had helped her doctor-husband fight. He, too, was long dead.

The fact that he had left Camp Chase should have been a relief. But the woman's harsh accent filled him with dread. He had never heard anyone speak like that before, not even in the prison. Was he with friends, or in a smaller, more lavish prison?

"He's awake?" he heard a younger voice from outside the door. Whereas the older woman sounded annoyed, this Gretchen sounded excited. "Has he said anything? Can we keep him?"

"Lord above, Gretchen," the older voice said. "You do not ask to keep a man the way children ask to keep a dog."

"Tante Klegg," Gretchen said, her laughter bubbling. "You know I don't mean it like that. It wouldn't be right to send him away, not when he needs our help."

"It is why he needs our help that I think he should go away," Tante Klegg said.

Footsteps padded toward the room.

He figured Gretchen must be barefoot. Too pained to move, he scanned the sparse room. Compared to Camp Chase, he felt spoiled.

The walls were rough log panels, whitewashed. Beside his bed was a rickety nightstand topped by a tin pitcher and cup. A chair was at the foot of his bed. Someone had put the remnants of his shoes below the chair and draped his tattered jacket on the seat. His haversack was nowhere in sight. The room had a single window, covered by a large piece of burlap. Above him was a posy of field flowers, hanging from a nail on the wall.

Nothing to tell me where I am, he thought, frustrated.

A fresh face peeked in the doorway. Gretchen's, he assumed. Two auburn braids swung past her shoulders. Her calico skirts were not as wide as Tante Klegg's. Gretchen smiled at him as if they were old friends and kept many secrets together.

He shrunk away. He had no friends but the man who sent him from the prison hospital.

"Don't worry," Gretchen said, stepping into the room. Her swaying full skirts revealed bare feet with dirt-speckled toes. She glanced behind her and dropped her voice to a whisper. "I didn't tell my aunt where you're from."

His eyes widened, wondering what she could know about where he was from. He rubbed his forehead. His fingers stopped when they touched a frayed fabric edge he did not remember. He glanced down at his pillow to find it bloodied.

Perhaps the people who had moved him to the straw tick bed had also bandaged his forehead. He hoped that he had not, in his muddled mind, told her he was a prisoner. So much for mercy... no doubt there was a local authority on the way now to take him back to camp.

Gretchen bit her lip, suppressing a grin. "This is exciting," she admitted, still whispering. She leaned close so he could hear. "I've never met a prisoner before."

All right, so he had told her he was a prisoner. He hoped he had passed out before saying much else.

"I'm not—" His voice cracked and he felt his cheeks burn. He cleared his throat while Gretchen poured water from the pitcher.

He noticed how Gretchen kept a hand in her skirts. It mimicked the way prison guards rested their hands on their hip holsters. War had changed the world if this slight young woman carried a weapon in her home, miles from any battle.

Gretchen handed him the tin cup, her brows raised. "You're not admitting you're a prisoner?" She crossed her arms and studied him.

He stared at the cup in his hand.

"It's not poisoned," she said.

"Don't see why I'd admit anything, ma'am, in my situation," he said before sipping.

Gretchen glanced at the door in case Tante Klegg appeared. "Well, you're determined to not make this easy," she said, frowning. "You told me you escaped from Camp Chase, so that's against you. And you don't look like any Union soldier I've seen walking to Columbus for mustering out. You might as well admit it. You're in no condition to go anywhere."

He glared at Gretchen over the cup's rim. If he were less exhausted, he would tell her a thing or two to wipe that smirk off her face. Who did she think she was?

Then he noticed her sleeve had blood on it. He figured it had to be his. Gretchen must have cradled his head, perhaps while bandaging it. He was in no position to show a temper; she was right about that.

"Why did you come to my farm? Why not leave on the trains with the other prisoners? It's in the newspapers. They're releasing people by the hundreds." Gretchen sat in the chair at the foot of his bed, resting her hands in her lap.

He remembered seeing her, too far away to make it worth the effort to call out. And then, she hovered over him, asking where he came from. And him admitting, like the fool he was, that he had escaped from Camp Chase.

"You don't like to talk much, do you?" Gretchen asked. She slipped her hand back into her skirts. "I told you I didn't tell my aunt where you came from, and I won't tell Mama, either. It would only get both of us in trouble."

He took another swig of water. "Why bother, then?"

Gretchen's head tilted. "For the adventure?"

"Adventure has a way of being nothing like you expect," he said.

Gretchen leaned back, having the nerve to pout. "Well, I did save you. And my Tante Klegg is too smart to say anything to anyone else until we know who you are." She waited for him to speak. "Well, come on then, who are you?"

He touched the bandage on his head. Maybe Gretchen was worth trusting.

"I'm..." He blinked at her, waiting for the words to come. He rubbed his eyes hard. His right ear began to hurt. A roaring noise crowded his brain. He was more tired than he thought.

Of course he knew his own name.

Gretchen's eyes narrowed. "You won't tell me?"

His mouth began to water, and he swallowed with a grimace. "I don't know it."

Her fists perched on her hips. "You must think I don't know beans."

He scratched the crown of his head, shifting the bandage. He patted it back in place. "Doc said I was in real trouble for a while. Maybe lost some of my mind from the fever."

"Which battle gave you the fever?" Gretchen asked. "Maybe we could find a newspaper and your name."

He shrugged, not sure it mattered. Those lists of living and dead and missing never got it right. He knew two men who had read of their deaths while in the prison! Fact was, they had sent him straight to the hospital barracks, and no one ever asked his name. Whoever called his name expecting an answer would have counted him among the dead by now.

"Well, I have to call you something. My aunt will insist you have a name. She's proper about things like that," Gretchen mused. She glanced at the door again, expecting Tante Klegg to appear any moment. "And my aunt will like you better if you're German."

"Are you German?" he asked, unsure how else to respond.

"Mama and Tante Klegg are, so, yes." Gretchen snapped her fingers. "We'll call you Karl. Karl is a steady German name." She stood, turning her back to him. "We'll say your mother is German, and your father is American, like me. Mama will have to take pity on you. You'll remind her of my brother."

"Tell falsehoods to your mother often, then?"

Gretchen paused, her hand on the doorknob. "When it suits me, why not? My aunt says I'm blessed with knowing souls. That has to count for something."

"How can you know the soul of a man who doesn't know his own name?" he scoffed.

"Gretchen!" Tante Klegg called. "Your mama wants to speak with you. Now."

Gretchen shook her head at Karl. "It's always now, now, now with Tante Klegg. You'll learn. Don't keep her waiting."

Karl blinked at the hem of Gretchen's sweeping skirts as she scampered away. *Should've stayed at the prison.*

'UNION' CELEBRATION

Saturday, 15 April 1865 / The Ohio Daily Statesman

The 'Union' Celebration, as it was called in the published programs, was opened at six o'clock yesterday morning by a salute of one hundred guns in Capitol Square, by the ringing of bells and the display of flags on public and private buildings.

A salute of one hundred guns was also fired at noon, and again at six o'clock in the evening. During the forenoon, the streets were generally empty and quiet; but in the afternoon, they began to be a little lively with people from the country and citizens promenading.

THREE

Saturday, 15 April 1865 / Grove City, Ohio

"Slow down," Gretchen heard her mother say to Tante Klegg. They were on the porch just outside the kitchen, which adjoined Werner's bedroom. "You know I cannot understand when you snarl."

Instead, Tante Klegg shouted, not bothering to translate from German. She pounded the wall with her fist.

Gretchen understood enough to know she should stop eavesdropping, unless she wanted more trouble.

Gretchen's mother sighed. "Why do you do this?" she asked. "We are in America. We are Americans. We should speak English."

Silence outside.

Gretchen imagined her mother, market basket in hand, and Tante Klegg, towering over her. She stoked the cooling stove fire so if they entered, she would look busy.

The silence continued, unnerving her. Usually, Tante Klegg would retort when her mother demanded she speak English. For Tante Klegg to remain silent could only mean she was too angry to say a word. Gretchen poked at the fire a little harder, hoping the next words out of Tante Klegg's mouth were not that they had found a prisoner and put him on Werner's bed.

Gretchen's mother had a terror of Confederates. She hoped when her mother saw Karl, she would change her mind. After all, Karl could hardly carry a tin cup. His eyes had the dazed brightness of a child woken from a nightmare and his forehead sweat with a light fever. His halting words and labored breathing emphasized his weakness.

Karl was too ill to harm anyone.

"Stop hiding," Tante Klegg said, raising her voice as if Gretchen could not hear her. "Come tell your mama what you have done."

Gretchen whispered a prayer for courage.

She heard Tante Klegg snort. "Praying will not help you!"

"Edelgard," her mother chided. She also raised her voice, since Gretchen had yet to walk outside. "Gretchen, come. Your Tante Klegg tells me you have done a terrible thing."

Gretchen smoothed her skirts so the revolver would be difficult to detect. No need to worry her mother before explaining things.

"Not a terrible thing, Mama," Gretchen said, walking outside.

"Annoying, then?" Her mother's hands rested on her stomach, and when she smiled, her nose crinkled. She never let her smiles for Gretchen reach her hazel eyes.

"I think for Tante Klegg, yes," Gretchen admitted. She dropped her gaze to her hem and clasped her hands behind her back.

Her aunt huffed, but she did not argue.

"Then you must tell me what you did. You have made it my problem to solve again, I think," her mother said. "And then I must tell you my news."

Gretchen paused at the sound of her mother's choked voice and looked up.

Her mother's eyes seemed bloodshot in the harsh afternoon shadows. She clasped her hands together and pulled them apart, suddenly seeming frantic enough to burst. She looked from Tante Klegg to Gretchen and back.

It had to be news about Papa. Or Werner. Gretchen pushed Tante Klegg aside and grabbed her mother. "What is it? Are they hurt?"

Tears welled in her mother's eyes and her mouth moved, but she made no sound.

"Stop sniveling, Adelaide," Tante Klegg said.

Gretchen's mother shook her head. "No, no, my news is not about them. I do not know if they are safe or dead! My son, what will come of him?"

Gretchen gripped tighter, glaring into her mother's face. "Papa and Werner will return; don't you dare say they've died."

Her mother stifled a sob behind pressed lips.

Gretchen softened her hold into a light hug. Her mother maintained her posture, refusing to lean into Gretchen's arms. "What is it, then?"

"Our president. He is dead!"

Gretchen exchanged a puzzled look with Tante Klegg. The war was over. President Lincoln and the Union were the victors. The newspaper had just shared his speech about reconciliation with their rebellious southern brothers. The president could not be dead. Someone must have been teasing her in the market.

"Where did you hear this? There was no news of his illness," Tante Klegg said.

Her mother's skin was a mottled red, her tidy hair falling from its careful coif. "Not illness! Murder." She did not give Gretchen or Tante Klegg time to understand. "Killed by an ungrateful, rascal Confederate sympathizer."

Gretchen's stomach churned. She wondered if she was about to taste her breakfast a second time.

"A Confederate killed the president?" Tante Klegg asked, glancing at the house.

Gretchen knew what she was thinking. They had just put a Confederate in Werner's bedroom. And he was not dead.

"What more is there to know?" her mother said. "A young man leaped at the president, shot him, and ran away. For all the papers know, he could be in Ohio by now!"

Tante Klegg threw a nasty, satisfied smile at Gretchen. The expression dashed her hopes of explaining "Karl" to her hysterical mother.

"I think it is time to tell your mother *your* news," Tante Klegg said to Gretchen. She took the trouble to sit on the porch steps.

"Do you not hear me, Edelgard?" Her mother advanced on her aunt. "The president is dead. Someone murdered him! The war will never end now, and we will never see Werner or Gregory again!"

Tante Klegg waved her sister's concerns away. "You worry about the wrong things, Adelaide. Ask your daughter what she has done, and you will see why it is important."

Gretchen froze.

"Tell me, then," her mother said, "if you think it is so important." In the awkward silence that followed, she studied Gretchen. "Is that blood on your sleeve? Werner?"

Gretchen snatched her mother's elbow to stop her. "No, no, Mama, not Werner, not anyone we know. He is not... from... this area."

Her mother stared at her, her expression darkening.

Gretchen gulped. "I think the young man is a rebel, Mama. I think he came from Camp Chase."

"A rebel!"

"He's fresh from Camp Chase, Mama. There is no way this man could have shot the president. He's weak. He's just a boy."

Her mother frowned, her brows scrunched together. "Boys know how to use guns, Gretchen, and this boy might have shot your Papa, or Werner."

Gretchen winced.

"Show me." Before Gretchen could stop her, her mother rushed into the kitchen. Her hoop skirts flew up, revealing dusty petticoats as she burst into Werner's bedroom.

Gretchen chased her, Tante Klegg close behind. They stumbled over each other trying to get into Werner's bedroom first.

"Get out of my son's bed," her mother shrieked, ripping the blanket from Karl.

Karl cowered, curling into a fetal position with big eyes as Gretchen's mother clawed at his thin frame.

"Mama, stop," Gretchen said, prying her mother from Karl. She looked at Tante Klegg for help, having never seen her mother so hysterical.

Tante Klegg watched from the doorway, arms crossed over her chest. "Adelaide, let go of the child."

"This is not a child. This is a man. And he is a Confederate. What more do we need to know? Have you sent for the sheriff?"

"Of course not," Gretchen said, panting. "He isn't dangerous. Look at him. He's shivering like a leaf."

Karl's teeth chattered and the old bed quaked with him. He watched Gretchen's mother as if his life depended on her. Perhaps it did.

"He does look pitiful," Gretchen's mother said.

"He *is* pitiful," Gretchen said, snatching the opportunity. "We had to carry him into the house. This can't be the man who shot the president."

Her mother did not take her gaze from the shaking Karl.

Karl glanced at Gretchen, beseeching and frightened.

"Think about it, Mama," Gretchen continued. "Why would he stay in Ohio? Wouldn't he go straight south?" She touched her mother's arm. "Mama, what if this was Werner, trying to get home to us? Wouldn't you want some girl to take care of him until he could make his way home?"

"Devilish child! Playing with my emotions like that!"

Tante Klegg entered the room to replace the blanket over Karl. "She is right, though, Adelaide. You would want Werner watched over."

Gretchen, surprised by Tante Klegg's endorsement, smiled at her. Tante Klegg's expression was thoughtful.

"This is true," Gretchen's mother admitted.

Somewhere in the distance, church bells began tolling.

"They are marking the death of the president," her mother whispered. "And we stand here with a man who might as well have done it himself."

Gretchen played with the end of her braid, looking from her mother to Karl to her aunt. President Lincoln had said everyone had to do his or her part to reconcile after the war. But Karl was a Confederate on the day President Lincoln died. Killed by some Confederate actor, her mother babbled.

Gretchen's eyes narrowed. She had never seen an actor, but she knew they were master liars. Their entire purpose was to lie to people, to make them believe what was not real. Karl could be pretending to not remember his name. He could be lying about having escaped Camp Chase. She had no idea how far she was from the nation's capital, but while it sounded impossible, there were trains to cross the country in a hurry.

Gretchen watched Karl as he hid under the blanket. She hoped she was right in thinking there was no way he could be the killer.

$100,000 REWARD

Thursday, 20 April 1865 / Washington City, District of Columbia

Major General Dix: The murderer of our late beloved President, Abraham Lincoln, is still at large.

$50,000 reward will be paid by this department for his apprehension, in addition to any reward offered by municipal authorities or State Executives.

$25,000 reward will be paid for the apprehension of A. C. Surratt, sometimes called Port Tobacco, one of Booth's accomplices.

$25,000 reward will be paid for any information that shall conduce to the arrest of either of the above named criminals or their accomplices.

All persons harboring or secreting the said person, or either of them, or aiding or assisting their concealment or escape, will be treated as accomplices in the murder of the President and the attempted assassination of the Secretary of State, and shall be subject to trial before a military commission and the punishment of death.

Let the stain of innocent blood be removed from the land by the arrest and punishment of the murderers. All good citizens are exhorted to aid public justice on this occasion. Every man should consider his own conscience charged with this solemn duty, and rest neither night nor day until it be accomplished.

[Signed] Edwin M. Stanton, Secretary of War.

FOUR

Saturday, 15 April 1865/ Grove City, Ohio

They were talking about him again. They were always talking about him. Always as if he were not there, the spiteful things. As if he could not hear their disgust and worry. He knew he was not the cleanest prisoner, but he had taken care to wash his face on occasion.

His head felt hot, so hot, and heavy, so heavy, and... red. He felt red. Could a person feel red? If they could, that was how he felt. Red, hot, heavy, wet. His eyes were wide, yet he could not see. That should worry him, but the blurred shapes soothed his aching head. He clutched his arms close and shivered. Seemed he was not quite over his fever spells. He dreaded the confusion that was certain to take over.

Female voices spoke, rather than the male voices he had grown accustomed to hearing. He was glad they had allowed women back into the prison. They were gentler with their poking and prodding to see if he was still alive. They tried to smile to bolster his hopes.

He looked up at a whitewashed ceiling. That was a nice touch. Made the small room seem bigger; all that white to bounce the sunlight around.

He could hear himself panting. He knew he did not have the breath to ask for medicine. He hoped maybe they could read his pained expression and relieve him without asking.

But no, the women had no time to look at him, other than to point at him and raise their voices. Arguing did not seem helpful for a hospital barracks. Not when they could go to the next man in the cot down the way. It was so quiet. Had all the other prisoners died? Maybe that was why they argued about him. He was the last one, and they were not sure what to do with him.

Oh, they were arguing whether he should stay? He could answer that question: no. He opened his mouth and felt his lip crack open. The sudden iron taste of blood startled him. He wondered when he last had water. He had been in the prison long enough for someone to give him water.

Water. The thought made him lick his lips and sigh the way other prisoners did when thinking about girls back home.

That was right; the young woman had given him a sip from a cup. He looked around for the cup, but with his unclear head, he had trouble finding it.

The voices rose an octave. He winced. If they did not want him in Camp Chase, that was fine by him. He did not want to stay anyway. Who would? Crowded, sweaty, muddy. All day, every day. Random gun shots in the night. Prisoners without an arm or leg or heart, shot because they were trying to light a fire in the frigid winter air.

But it was not winter anymore. He had walked in hot, humid weather. His lip bled from being so parched. It was April, springtime; time for Pa to try to pull him from school again.

He struggled to remember if Pa had planted the crops already, or if there had been a late frost. Or was it last year that had the late frost? No, that could not be right. Last year he had been on the battlefield. But not this year either, since this year was this year. He had not gone to school, because he had not been home, because he had been in a prison.

It had been so long since he had been home. And even when he was home he was not home, though he was not sure how that worked.

Home. That was where he wanted to be, but nobody wanted him there. That was why he had gone off to war. At least that was how he remembered it, sort of. Signed up to escape a lack of wanting and needing him. He had to belong somewhere, so perhaps he belonged on the battlefield.

"*Mein Gott*," one of the women said. The older one. The angry one. "He has lost his mind."

He squeezed his eyes shut and blinked. There was that harsh accent again. Almost made it sound as if he had regained his voice and just maybe had been talking all this time.

That was unfortunate if true. He had no idea what he was blabbering about. His mind was every which way, and then some, which seemed like a lot of ways to....

He licked his lip again and tasted that familiar cold tang of iron. Lips chapped and bleeding, but at least his blood was warm and flowing, not cool and sticky.

"Make him stop," said the younger woman, the one who looked like the angry one, only not so angry.

But the younger woman had yelled and clawed at him. She had ripped his blanket away. Perhaps she was the angry one. No, that did not seem fair. The older woman looked angry always. The younger woman looked angry because of a sad situation. Now that was a clever thought, insightful on his part, he felt: angry because of sadness.

"Mama, he's fevered," said the youngest of all, the one who kept a hand in her pocket like a man keeping a hand on his holster.

Oh yes, she must have a gun. She must be ready to shoot. Why would she not just shoot? It would end the argument, and maybe he would be in a home better than any he could find on earth.

"He doesn't know what he's saying. You don't know what you're saying," the youngest said to him.

She said her name was Gretchen. That was right, Gretchen. He would hold onto that. Gretchen. And she had given him a name. Karl. Yes, Karl, a good German name, because she said he had to have a German mother.

That sounded comforting. Karl thought he liked the idea of a German mother. He could have a good German mother who would make sausages. He would eat the sausages in the casing. A horse was dead beneath him on the battlefield. He saw sausage links rolling from its stomach. Not appetizing when the sausages steamed like that, still connected to a dying body.

"Don't shoot me," he screamed.

"I'm not going to shoot you," Gretchen said, but even she did not sound convinced.

"Who gave you a gun?" Her mother backed away.

"Papa did," Gretchen said, "because he knew you wouldn't use it."

"Give it to me, I will use it," the oldest of all retorted. Tante Klegg; that was her name. A harsh name for a harsh woman. Karl decided he did not like Tante Klegg.

"And that's the other reason why Papa gave me the gun," Gretchen shot back, "because he knew you would use it."

Gretchen's logic did not make sense, but Karl liked it anyway. Her logic made the angry one, Tante Klegg, quiet.

"Let me see it," said Gretchen's mother. He did not know her name.

"I'm not going to reveal my weapon before I'm good and ready to use it, Mama," Gretchen said.

Karl felt a goofy grin spreading across his face.

"What if we die because he shot the president?" Tante Klegg said.

"He's feverish and weak. I wouldn't worry," Gretchen said.

"Hey now," Karl said. That time, he knew he spoke, and he knew what he said while speaking. Perhaps the fever confusion was passing. "I can shoot an apple off a galloping horse!"

"Oh?" Gretchen asked, her frustration forgotten, her eyes alight with curiosity and maybe even a challenge.

"Gretchen, this is a stranger in your brother's bed. Not a new shooting partner," Tante Klegg said. "You forget yourself and your time. We are at war with this boy."

"No, we're not," Gretchen said, whipping out her revolver, finally.

Karl scooted back in the bed. His entire body cringed. His face flushed with shame. A real soldier, a real man, would not have cringed, or cowered, or wished all this would just stop.

Gretchen's mother screamed and threw her hands to her mouth. She stared at Gretchen as if she were a stranger.

Tante Klegg crossed her arms. The only hint to Karl of her alarm was that one of her eyebrows rose.

Karl took another look at the revolver in Gretchen's hand. She pointed it at the puncheon floor. It still had the safety set and the hammer unlocked. He looked at Tante Klegg, who watched him with a calculating expression. He had the eerie feeling she knew what he did, that Gretchen was just being dramatic.

"We aren't at war anymore," Gretchen said.

Karl heard the undercurrent charging Gretchen's voice. She attempted to sound calm and in control, even though she knew she was neither.

"Mr. Lincoln said, 'old as well as new, north as well as south.' He said that. He said it in Columbus, before the war, before he was even president." Gretchen paused. "He said it, and he meant it, and Papa and Werner surely wouldn't have gone to war if they didn't believe it. We're all in this together. Otherwise, we all have to be at war."

Gretchen talked in circles, which was about how the room was spinning.

"Yes," Tante Klegg said. "Look where that landed him. His pretty words landed him where it lands everyone."

Tante Klegg watched Karl with that calculating expression. Her dark eyes were unnerving. It took forever for her to blink.

Karl wondered whether Germans believed in witches. He wondered whether he believed in witches. Perhaps Tante Klegg was a witch. He wondered if that belief had any effect on whether Tante Klegg could harm him with her powers.

Tante Klegg's expression hid behind guns in a frigid field trying to decide who would shoot first. He never did. He never shot first. It made no sense that he was alive, knowing he never shot first. It made no sense that he was in a strange bed, pestered by strange women who shouted about dead presidents.

Karl shook his head. "Which one?" His voice warbled, but otherwise was clear.

The women stared at him as if he had lost his mind. Well, he might have. No, he had. He could not remember his own name now, could he?

"Which one what?" Gretchen said.

Karl gulped, not believing Gretchen did not know what he was asking. A girl who talked in circles could think in circles, which was all Karl could do at the moment. And here he had thought they were so alike. Neither was keen on the war continuing, that much he knew.

"Which president?" Karl asked. He wiped sweat from his brow before it stung his eyes. "Which president died?"

Gretchen's mother drew up to her full, if short, height. Her blue eyes sparked, and the corner of her mouth twitched. "*The* president has died. There is only one."

Karl hugged the blanket tighter around his shoulders. Davis or Lincoln, Lincoln or Davis? He was always hearing those names in the prison. Debates and chants and all sorts of nonsense, always rallying, though to what, he never knew. To death, perhaps, since that was how it ended for most in a war. What glory was death? Death was an escape from trudging through mud and gnawing on moldy, maggoty hardtack.

Karl rubbed his forehead again. He did not understand why he could remember details like that, but not his name, his home, or his family. So he held onto the names he could remember. President Lincoln and President Davis. President Lincoln. President Davis. Lincoln. Davis. Union. Confederate. Dead. Alive.

It took Karl a moment to realize everyone was staring at him, horrified. He had not been chanting in his head.

"There is no such thing as a President Davis," Tante Klegg said, her voice piercing him.

Karl frowned.

"Why are we watching over this fool?" Gretchen's mother demanded, waving her hand at him. "He does not even know which president is worth mourning!"

"I would guess he didn't know the war ended this week. Or in our favor," Gretchen said.

Well, she was right about that. Karl had not known the war was over. He certainly had not known the Confederacy had lost. Other soldiers, the ones in the prison and on the trains, were no doubt disheartened by such news. He felt a weight lift his shoulders. He almost did not recognize what he felt was relief.

"So President Davis died?" Karl asked, tentative.

Tante Klegg threw her hands up to the ceiling and rolled her eyes.

"President Lincoln died," Gretchen's mother said, "at the hand of one of your kind."

Karl did not care for Mr. Lincoln, but he did not think that made him against Mr. Lincoln, either. Even at Camp Chase, Karl had avoided the debates about how the war would end. Prisoners were unsure the Confederacy could win despite the encouragement from home.

Karl could only remember thinking it was a shame he was missing it. Not the shooting and killing. There was something just beyond his reach. He knew he was missing something. He had an assignment to do.

"He does not show remorse or any mourning!" Gretchen's mother said.

"That's not a sign of guilt, Mama," Gretchen was quick to say.

"Perhaps," Tante Klegg said, "but we have nothing to say he is not guilty. Except your belief that he is too ill to have done it."

Gretchen tucked her revolver in her pocket. Postures relaxed. "We're wasting our time talking about this," she said.

"I am sorry to hear Mr. Lincoln passed on," Karl said. He sounded as polite as a pastor. He might as well have said he was sorry to hear the neighbor's dog had dug up the flowers. "But I don't understand. Killed by one of my kind?" He rubbed his head, pausing when his fingers hit a thick bandage. "A prisoner?"

"A Confederate!" Gretchen's mother said, leaping forward with her hands out ready to strangle him. Tante Klegg grabbed one of her arms, throwing her off balance. They tripped and fell to the ground in a pile of shrieks and skirts.

Karl stared at them, seeing more ankles than he ever had in his entire life. He felt his face bloom with embarrassment and he averted his gaze to the ceiling. "If you think I... if you believe I'm... well, what am I doing in your house?"

Gretchen's mother and aunt paused untangling their skirts to glare at her.

"You're not helping," Gretchen said to Karl through gritted teeth. She cleared her throat. "If you're guilty, then we've captured the murderer. We're heroes. We stopped the war from continuing because we'll have stopped the last spirit of hope for the rebels."

Karl's stomach dropped. He was glad his stomach was empty; otherwise, he would have emptied it all over his pillow. Karl did not remember much before Camp Chase. He did know he had not wanted the war to continue. He had been almost glad they sent him to prison because it meant fewer bullets whizzing past his head. "How would killing Mr. Lincoln continue the war?"

Gretchen's mother took her arm to pull herself to standing. She slapped the dust from her skirts. "I do not care if he murdered the president. I want him out of my house." She left in the same whirl of skirts that brought her there in the first place.

Tante Klegg continued to watch Karl from where she sat on the floor. "He does not act like a soldier."

Karl wondered how she could know that, and why a part of him agreed.

"So you will let me keep him?" Gretchen asked. She held out her hand to help her aunt.

"This is Gregory Miller's house, not mine." Tante Klegg grunted as Gretchen hefted her from the floor.

Karl figured that was Gretchen's father.

"And as he handed you the revolver, it seems you are responsible." Tante Klegg moved to the doorway, her expression thoughtful as a clock chimed. "I am interested to know how you intend to explain him to Alina."

Had he the energy, Karl would have laughed at Gretchen's stricken expression. Something about this "Alina" deflated Gretchen.

These women were too secretive, too complicated. And they thought he had shot a president!

FIVE

Saturday, 15 April 1865 / Grove City, Ohio

That was just like Tante Klegg to offer hope and snatch it away with a well-placed cackle.

Gretchen knew she should listen to her elders with a simpering smile. And she would, once she stopped wanting to shout her frustration at them.

First, Gretchen needed to clean Karl's wounds. Earlier, she only had enough time to wrap his head.

Gretchen tucked auburn strands of hair into her braids before bending to carry a small basin of water. She had a cloth draped over her arm, and she made sure Werner's door was open for propriety. Karl was asleep. His entire body shook from fever, but he did not wake when Gretchen wiped his brow.

Gretchen wondered how she could have ever mistaken him for her brother. They both had dark hair that shone amber in sunlight. They both had piercing eyes that made one believe they saw exactly what one did not wish them to see. That was where the similarities stopped.

It had been years since Gretchen had seen Werner. She remembered him walking from the farm, hand waving. His cheeks were full, his hair shining, his smile broad.

Karl's sunken cheeks, blood-matted hair, and raspy breathing sent a chill through Gretchen. She wondered what conditions her brother suffered.

The more Gretchen dabbed at Karl's forehead, the more pressure she felt building in her throat. She shook her head, determined not to cry. What did she, a fifteen-year-old girl, know about taking care of an ill soldier?

Gretchen splashed her hand into the basin. She swished the cloth around before rubbing away the dirt on Karl's chin. Water dripped onto her skirts, but she was already unkempt, sweaty, and frazzled. She doubted her mother would notice.

Soon half of Karl's face was clean. He might have been handsome once, before his illness and war experiences. His tanned skin hinted at walking in the sun for who knew how long. A peek under his collar showed him pale otherwise.

Gretchen paused. The idea of harboring and caring for Karl had been exciting until the news of Mr. Lincoln's death. Now Gretchen ran the risk of being his compatriot, his *confederate*. She did not want to be the young woman who nursed Mr. Lincoln's killer back to life.

At the same time, Gretchen did not think Karl could be the murderer. Tante Klegg was right. There was something... unsoldierly about Karl. Not that Gretchen knew a whole lot about soldiers. He looked frail, for one thing. And his fevered eyes gave him an innocence that made her question whether he ever had put a bullet through a body.

Karl was observant, though. Gretchen saw how his focus darted around the room, as if he were cataloging everything in sight. Yet he lacked the sharp reflexes she expected from a kill-or-be-killed life.

Rather than snatching the revolver from her hand, Karl shrank into Werner's blanket. Karl avoided confrontation, instead of facing it like a murderer on the run.

Gretchen frowned. It could be that acting frail and weak was part of Karl's plan, only to shoot them all in their sleep. She twisted the cloth so the water did not drip all over Werner's blanket.

Karl would not attack her family. Not on her watch. Gretchen resolved to sleep outside Werner's door for good measure. Karl would have to trip and face her revolver before reaching her aunt and mother.

Gretchen unwrapped the bandage around Karl's head and dabbed at his hairline. The cut was minor, thank goodness. She was about to clean his ears and neck when the sound of insistent knocking stopped her mid-swipe.

Tante Klegg poked her head into the bedroom. "Alina."

Gretchen jumped to her feet, dropping the bloodied cloth to the floor. She had already forgotten. "What do we do?"

Tante Klegg nodded at Karl's feet. "We carry him to the barn." She grabbed his shoulders so Gretchen could wrap her arms around his thin torso. Tante Klegg took his feet, and they lifted him from the bed.

"How will we sneak him past her?" Gretchen whispered.

"Adelaide will take her to the creek."

Gretchen nodded. The creek was where Werner had proposed to Alina. She never protested whenever someone suggested taking a walk there.

Gretchen hefted Karl a little higher, ignoring his fevered mumbling. She peeked out of the doorway and could hear nothing.

Tante Klegg and Gretchen shuffled across the room and into the kitchen. They called it their kitchen, but it was also their main living space. Gretchen panted, her fingers slipping. She grimaced, wondering why she carried the heavy part.

"Do not make faces at me. Be glad I help at all," Tante Klegg said.

Gretchen's jaw jutted forward. She focused on navigating around the table. With each step, she feared Alina would burst into view.

The log house was simple: two bedrooms off the kitchen and a tight stairwell up to the large attic. Gretchen avoided her parents' bedroom, angling instead for the door to the back porch.

By this point, Gretchen was in a full-body sweat. She made Tante Klegg pause so she could put Karl down. When she picked him up again, it was with his back facing hers. She looped her arms under his and stumbled down the porch steps.

Gretchen knew it took forty-seven steps to reach the barn from the porch. She kept stepping on sharp twigs and shifting pebbles.

"Keep your balance," Tante Klegg said. "If we drop him and he makes a noise, Alina will notice."

The creek was far enough away that all Gretchen could see was Alina's gray skirt flapping in the breeze.

"I doubt she'll hear a thing," Gretchen said. She wriggled so Karl's rump settled onto her lower back.

By the time they settled Karl atop a pile of old straw in an empty horse stall, Gretchen could hardly breathe. Her braids were in shambles. She knew her sweat left large stains beneath her arms. And she had gotten more of Karl's blood on her, though she did not know how.

They could hear Alina and her mother returning from the creek.

Punctual to a fault, Alina visited the house at three every day, and after church on Sundays. It was her way of ensuring that when Werner returned, everything would continue as it had before the war.

"Change your dress and wash your face," Tante Klegg said, throwing a pile of fabric at Gretchen from a hook nearby.

Gretchen stared at the dress in her hands. This was her Sunday best, the only other dress she owned. "When did you put this in the barn?"

Tante Klegg tsked and waved her hand. "I keep time. I knew we would have trouble with Alina."

"Yes, but why help me?" Gretchen's voice trailed off when Tante Klegg abandoned her to greet Alina. Gretchen shrugged. She would never understand her aunt.

Karl sighed and snuggled into the straw as if it were a pile of down feathers. Gretchen shook her head and grabbed an old horse blanket to drape over him. He still shivered. While the blanket was filthy, it would hide him should anyone else stumble into the barn.

Gretchen made sure to swing the horse stall door shut so Karl could not see her if he woke. She re-braided her hair and splashed her face with water from a bucket.

Alina was always offering advice about her appearance. It made Gretchen run crazy as a loon. Unlike Alina, she had more important things to worry about, like a prisoner in her barn.

Gretchen corrected herself. It was more than keeping a prisoner in her barn. She had kept a Confederate in Werner's bedroom, in his bed, no less. Gretchen had a feeling that Alina knowing about Karl would go over as well as it had with her mother and aunt.

Gretchen entered the kitchen, striving to seem as if she had not locked a Confederate in the barn. She kept her hands at her waist, the way her mother taught her. It was only when her mother glared at her feet that Gretchen realized she had forgotten to put on her shoes. Gretchen swallowed a sigh. Where Alina was demure by default, Gretchen had to think about it.

Alina sat at the kitchen table with Gretchen's aunt and mother. "Gretchen," she said, "my *Mütter* Miller tells me you have heard the awful news about the president."

Alina had claimed Gretchen's mother as her own after Werner's proposal, even though her mother still lived. Her accent matched her mother's and Tante Klegg's more than Gretchen's. Both her parents were Palatine Germans whereas Gretchen's father was American.

"Yes, awful," Gretchen said, sitting beside her mother.

Gretchen was careful not to look Tante Klegg in the eye. It was difficult since they sat across from one another. She was uncertain why her aunt had helped her move Karl. It felt funny to think of the word "grateful" in connection with Tante Klegg.

"My father fell to his knees to pray. I offered to fan him while he worked, but he insisted I keep my appointment with you," Alina continued. She perched her bonnet, decorated with fresh lilacs and grosgrain ribbon, in her lap. Her dainty fingers flitted past her temple to brush aside an errant hair that Gretchen could not see.

Alina was everything Gretchen was not: gentle, subservient, dainty. Alina was so sweet, if her mother and aunt were in the room. It was infuriating.

Gretchen's mother reached across the table to pat Alina's hand. The distance between Gretchen and her mother, though they sat side-by-side, was palpable. Gretchen gritted her teeth more with each pat her mother gave to Alina.

"Who do you think would do such a terrible thing?" Alina asked, looking from one woman to the next.

Tante Klegg leaned toward Alina with an awful sparkle in her eye. "Who do *you* think would do such a thing?"

Gretchen fidgeted.

"Honestly, I do not care to know. Those who do such things deserve to die," Alina said.

Gretchen almost fell out of her chair. Alina cried whenever Werner killed a spider. "You can't mean that."

"You do not speak for everyone, Gretchen," her mother said.

"You must forgive my sister. She is so enthusiastic about topics she cannot understand," Alina said.

"You have no idea how I struggle with her," Gretchen's mother said.

"You must forgive her simple thoughts," Alina said. "It is the reason why I love her so; you mustn't be angry with her."

Simple thoughts? Gretchen had never experienced an explosion before, but she had read of it once in a newspaper. The shattering pressure at her temple must be how an explosion felt. She shoved her hands into her pockets and snaked one ankle around the other beneath her skirts. If Gretchen did not hold herself down, she was going to wring Alina's neck once and for all. No matter the consequences if—that is, when—Werner returned.

"It is Gretchen's belief that we must look to the Confederates as misguided brothers, ja?" Alina said with a little laugh. "It is charming. Innocent and sweet." Her expression darkened, and she held Gretchen's mother's hand a little tighter. "But to think that one of these misguided brothers shot the man my uncle fought for, died for..."

Gretchen winced. In all the excitement, she had forgotten about Alina's daily visit, and worse, that Alina's uncle had died in the war. He had been one of the Grove City men to sign up during the first call for arms. There had been so many volunteers that many had to wait to sign up later, when the war was more desperate.

Alina's uncle and others from Jackson Township paid for patriotism with their lives, as had poor Mr. Lincoln. Gretchen wondered how far she would go for her country.

Gretchen's mother elbowed her. Not knowing what she wanted, Gretchen frowned. She frowned deeper when her mother mouthed, "Comfort her. She is your sister."

The last thing Gretchen wanted was to console Alina, who dabbed large tears from her bright eyes. Gretchen leaned closer to Alina anyway. She would do anything to keep the topic away from Karl. She reminded herself that her mother did not know that Karl was still on their land.

"Your uncle was a hero," Gretchen said. She refused to touch Alina, who watched her with a wary expression. "He died with honor, and that doesn't change because Mr. Lincoln died. The Union still won the war."

Her mother cleared her throat, trying to mask her surprise. Even Tante Klegg seemed a little impressed. Gretchen hoped that would translate into helping rather than antagonizing. Alina seemed even more wary.

On a normal day, after confirming there was no word from Werner, Alina would leave. Yet she remained at the table.

Gretchen could feel the sweat gathering at her temple. It was a hot day. She had spent hours fighting weeds before carrying Karl into and out of the house only to hide him in the barn. She wanted Alina to leave. She wanted to make sure Karl remained in the barn. She hoped she would be the only one to notice if he limped away.

Gretchen looked out the window, in case. Karl was not there, but the thought of him waking and revealing his presence made her want to retch.

Gretchen could see now this was not the time or place for adventure. Mr. Lincoln was dead. Alina's uncle was dead. Gretchen did not know if her brother and father lay injured, dead, or dying. Her mother was hysterical, and her aunt stoic. She had an unknown Confederate in her barn, sleeping under an old horse blanket next to her dirty dress.

"What are they doing in town to recognize the president's passing?" her mother asked Alina. She shifted her body so even though she sat beside Gretchen, her back was turned.

The movement was not lost on Gretchen, and she could feel her face grow hot. Her polite mother was doing her best to cut her out of the conversation. She glanced at Tante Klegg, who shook her head once. As always with Tante Klegg, Gretchen had no idea how to interpret that.

Alina was happy to change the subject back to her gossip. She described the black swaths of fabric hanging from the stores in Grove City, all two of them, and even the tavern. How people stopped their daily routines to hold one another while wondering what was to come.

Alina spoke around the issue, but all four women knew what she chose not to say. Everyone was gathering together because they did not know what else to do. They gathered because it hurt less to hear of some opportunistic Confederate attack if they heard it together.

No one wanted the war to continue. With the death of the president, and the Confederacy wounded and bitter, it was possible the war could continue.

The shriek from the barn personified that fear.

LYING IN STATE

Tuesday, 18 April 1865 / The Ohio Daily Statesman

PRESIDENT LINCOLN'S BODY LYING IN STATE—THOU-SANDS OF PERSONS VISIT THE EXECUTIVE MANSION.

The body of the late President is lying in state in the east room; thousands of persons of both sexes are thronging the avenue. The east room is decorated with the trappings of woe. In the immediate center of this spacious room is erected the catafalque, and the coffin is within the immediate view of the line of spectators.

Each person stops a moment to take a view of the face of the deceased, and many shed tears. The hands of friendship and affection have contributed the choicest flowers to adorn the coffin and make up the foundation upon which it rests.

Between half past nine this morning and noon at least 3,000 persons had visited the Executive Mansion, and thousands more slowly following in turn to indulge a similar privilege.

SIX

Saturday, 15 April 1865 / Grove City, Ohio

Karl opened his eyes, blinking in the darkness. He sat up with an awful start to the rich scent of cool, aged wood and musty body odor. He assumed the latter must be his own stench, which he paid no mind. For a panicked moment, he thought he was back at Camp Chase, but like earlier, the smells did not match. Sure, he smelled wood and hay, but there were other smells, different ones from the last time he woke.

The tut-tutting of chickens overhead explained the acrid coop smell. Karl knew plenty of men who would have killed to get those chickens. He was not one of those men, not when chickens came with those smells.

"Got to stop waking where I don't know where I am."

He sniffed the horse blanket covering him and recoiled. He kicked it off, gagging.

Karl still had no idea what his name was, so he noted what he knew with certainty. He was in a barn. Sweat drenched his body. His head throbbed. His stomach complained. His bare feet stung like the dickens. The chickens smelled bad. He sat on straw; it pricked through his threadbare clothing.

Karl shifted, trying to measure the size of the room. It was long but narrow, bounded by short walls and a padlocked door. The walls and door cleared the floor by a couple of inches, not enough to escape. He found a pile of fabric on the other side of the door and threw it over his shoulder. Perhaps those women had left him with replacement clothing.

He took a deep breath and choked on a chicken feather.

Karl felt the fabric slip from his shoulder, which is when he noticed how much there was... and there was a lot.

Karl felt around the floor again for the fabric, suspicious. The amount of fabric was far too much for a pair of pants or a shirt. He picked it up, curiosity giving way to horror.

There were sleeves, a dainty collar, small buttons down a front bodice. A tiny waist. Yards upon yards of fabric that could only make a skirt.

Face hot, Karl dropped the dress as if it were on fire.

A low moan came from the stall beside him.

Karl rubbed the back of his neck, his mouth dry. "Who's there?"

All he could hear was breathing.

"Is this... your... dress?" His voice dropped to a hoarse whisper. There was a horrible silence. Karl could feel his heart in his throat.

"Want it back?" Karl shook his head and said to himself, "Of course you'd like it back. Stupid I even mentioned it."

Karl grunted, frustrated it was taking so long for his eyes to adjust in the dim light. His mind raced with possibilities. He was not sure of anything these days, and this was the most lucid he had felt in weeks.

He could not stand the silence, and he tried again.

"If I did… anything untoward," Karl said, "please, accept my—my apologies." He ran his hand down his face and exhaled. "I've—I've been out of my head so long, it feels funny to be in my head."

A soft moan, this time sounding far less human.

Karl looked up to find huge doleful eyes staring at him from above the wall dividing his stall from hers. He could not help it. He shrieked.

Somewhere else, behind a thick wall, he heard the chickens cackle and caw in response to his panic. Large nostrils blew hot air in his face. Karl rubbed his eyes.

Details came into focus. The log-slatted wall separating them stood about chest-high. His barn-mate, a cow, angled her neck around the wall, trying to see him. Karl's laugh, while relieved, held a slight edge of hysteria. "Hey there," he said, his voice shaking.

Big eyelashes swept across high cheekbones. She crooned as if they were having a conversation.

"Wouldn't happen to know whose dress I'm holding?" Karl asked, not expecting an answer.

The cow huffed and turned away.

Karl began dragging his fingers along the dirt floor for a stick he could use to pick or break the padlock. He did not spend all that time in prison to end up in another one. He paused, panting. All this movement was exhausting.

Breaking the padlock was not the answer. He turned instead to study the hinges, but the barn door burst open, blinding him.

He stumbled back, arm thrown up to shield his eyes.

"What have you done?" he heard Tante Klegg say.

Karl dropped his arm. "What?"

"You screamed. You frightened our guest."

Tante Klegg was not the sort of woman to tell a falsehood to, not with her formidable silhouette blocking the only way out. Her hands rested at the apex of her wide skirts, and she did not bother to enter.

"There was something breathing and moaning. It turned out to be a cow, but I didn't expect her face so close..." Karl's voice trailed off. He could hear how ridiculous he sounded.

"You are in a barn."

He felt the back of his neck grow hot. "Y'all left me alone in the dark with strange noises and smells. What was I supposed to think?"

"That you are a man, and cows are not frightening to a man who has survived a war."

Karl clamped his mouth shut before he said anything that made her any more huffed. If Tante Klegg was anything like Gretchen, she hid a revolver and was ready to shoot him right there. No one would miss a dead Confederate in the middle of Ohio.

"We hid you for our safety," Tante Klegg explained while unlocking the stall.

Karl nodded, then frowned. "Our safety?"

She ignored his question. "What is that you hold?" Tante Klegg's voice grew colder. "Is that Gretchen's dress?" She bent to snatch it from the floor by his feet.

Karl's mouth went dry.

"What have you done?" Tante Klegg said.

He blanched. "Don't know."

"This is Gretchen's dress," she insisted, shaking it at him. When he stared at her, she ran her hand down her face, rambling on in German. "*Dummkopf*," he heard Tante Klegg say more than once.

"How did that end up in here with me?" Karl said, gesturing to the dress in her hand.

She sighed and a sinking feeling settled in Karl's gut.

"You must stay," Tante Klegg announced.

"Meaning I had the chance to leave?" he said. They both knew how far he would have gotten with his shaking limbs, dizziness, empty stomach, and bare feet.

Tante Klegg folded the dress until it was a square package, but even that could not hide the blood from view. His blood.

"I do not know what has happened, but you cannot leave. My foolish Gretchen changed in here..." She descended into a string of German again. "I meant her to change behind the barn or the outhouse. Foolish, stupid girl!"

A frisson of pain struck Karl's temple. He winced. He was ready to crawl back into the stall and sleep until this family forgot all about him.

Tante Klegg smiled. It was terrifying, and he wished she would stop. "Yes. This will be *sehr gut*. It will be penance."

"Beg pardon?" Karl said. "Penance for whom?"

SEVEN

Saturday, 15 April 1865 / Grove City, Ohio

Gretchen stood by the kitchen window, her revolver in hand. The kitchen was silent but for her mother's nervous sipping. Alina twisted her handkerchief, wondering who shrieked, or where, or why. She opened her mouth and shut it again.

"She's coming back," Gretchen announced, watching Tante Klegg step out of the barn.

"Is she hurt?" Alina whispered.

"No, but..." Gretchen squinted into the sunlight. "She's carrying something."

Oh. Oh no. Gretchen knew exactly what her aunt carried. She slammed the door shut and scooted back to her chair. She was not about to admit Tante Klegg was holding her dress. Not to Alina and not to her mother of all people. Not when they had heard a man scream from that direction.

"What took her so long? Are you sure she is safe?" Alina pressed.

Gretchen's mother seemed serene but her eyes flashed. She had realized they had only moved Karl, not removed him from the farm.

Not knowing what to say, Gretchen reset the safety on the revolver and slipped it into her pocket. She had not brandished her weapon as many times during the war as she had this morning.

Tante Klegg kicked the door open. Alina screamed. Gretchen stared at her sweaty, bloodied dress bundled in Tante Klegg's arms. Her mother rolled her eyes at all the dramatics, as if she had not been hysterical an hour before.

"Stop that," Tante Klegg said to Alina as she shut the door behind her.

Alina huffed, throwing a hand to her chest. "I heard a man scream as if he were dying, Tante Klegg. That is cause for me to be nervous."

"Hysterical, not nervous," Tante Klegg said. "Had you been nervous, you would have watched the barn when I entered it, you would have watched when I left. You would have found methods to protect yourself. You did none of these things. You are not nervous. You are hysterical."

Tante Klegg's tone made the word "hysterical" sound like the word "useless."

Alina's lower lip trembled. "You are so harsh."

"Try living with her," Gretchen said.

Tante Klegg ignored them, dropping Gretchen's dress into the bucket beside the stove.

"What is that?" her mother demanded. "It is filthy. Get it out of my house."

Gretchen frowned at Tante Klegg, begging. She knew where Tante Klegg had found that dress, somewhere in the stall with Karl. Gretchen felt her face inflame.

If only Alina had left! Then Gretchen could explain she had not changed in front of Karl, that she was not loose. She had thrown the dress near the stall so if someone wandered into the barn, they would not notice it. Seeing the dress in Tante Klegg's hands made Gretchen think she should have thrown it in the old pig sty.

Alina leaned forward, trying to see around Gretchen. "It looks like..." She glanced at Gretchen and fell silent.

"It is Gretchen's dress." Tante Klegg's tone was matter-of-fact.

Gretchen sighed. The adventure was over, having not lasted long in the first place. Once again, everyone would blame her for everything. Alina would have to know the secret now. Gretchen would have to fight to keep Karl again.

Alina frowned at Gretchen, but directed her question at Gretchen's mother. "*Mütter*, what was Gretchen's dress doing in the barn? That is an odd place to keep clothing."

Gretchen's mother lifted a shoulder and sipped her water. "I do not explain her. You know that."

"This must be why Gretchen is wearing her best dress," Alina mused. "Gretchen never wears her Sunday best, even for special occasions."

"That's not true," Gretchen protested. "I wore it six days ago."

"Sunday was six days ago," Alina said.

Tante Klegg picked up the water pail. "This is a family matter, Alina. Do not concern yourself."

Gretchen watched her aunt, too afraid to ask, too annoyed to object.

"Gretchen's clothing is a family matter too private for me to concern myself about?" Alina asked. "I'm practically her sister; I'm Werner's..." Her lip trembled again, accompanied this time by tears.

"Gretchen, go to Werner's room," Tante Klegg said. She placed a pot on the stove and went through the motions of stoking the flame. "Return with pants and a shirt. Suspenders if you find any."

"Are we washing early?" Gretchen asked, delaying the inevitable.

"Is that blood on her dress?" Alina asked, standing from her seat. "Gretchen, why is there blood on your dress?"

Alina looked at Tante Klegg. "Why do you want her to get Werner's clothing? Has my Werner returned?" The hope in her voice made Gretchen cringe.

"It is not Werner who needs the clothing," Tante Klegg said, her face red from stoking the flames. She straightened and turned, hands on her hips. Gretchen never liked when Tante Klegg stood like that. It meant she was about to say something certain to make Gretchen's life that much more difficult.

"It is for a soldier, but not Werner," Tante Klegg said. "Gretchen found him."

Gretchen's mother inhaled, her nostrils flaring. "Edelgard! You have no right to do this."

Tante Klegg was impassive as she filled a pot with water to soak the bloodstained dress. "I will not repeat the past," she said to no one.

Alina rounded on Gretchen. "A soldier! You found a soldier! Was he in Werner's volunteers? Has he news of Werner? What does he know of soldiers returning home? Why is he in the barn?" She grabbed Gretchen's hands from across the table. "You must tell me everything."

Gretchen squirmed.

"Yes," her mother taunted. "Tell her everything. What is his name?"

Gretchen swallowed. "Well... I call him... Karl..."

Her aunt dropped the pot on the stove and her mother hissed. "You call him Karl?" her mother turned an unseemly shade of purple. "That is our papa's name, you little..."

"Adelaide," Tante Klegg said, whipping around from the stove.

"Oh, Karl, that is a good strong name for a soldier," Alina interrupted with an annoying little sigh. "He knows of Werner's return, he must! Why else would he come to your farm?"

Gretchen closed her eyes. "His... we had to bandage his head. It affects his mind. He... doesn't seem to remember things."

Alina frowned. "Is he dangerous?"

Gretchen shook her head, having no idea.

"When will I meet him?" Alina asked, looking from one woman to another.

"Not today," Tante Klegg said. "He needs to rest."

Alina nodded. "Poor soul."

"You have no idea," Gretchen said. She narrowed her eyes at Tante Klegg, wondering what her aunt would say next. She hoped it would be to tell Alina to get out.

One thing was certain, and that was when Alina left, all Grove City would know Karl was at their farm.

Who knew how long Karl would stay in Grove City? For all they knew, he would escape at the first opportunity. He might have left already.

"We will see you at church tomorrow," Tante Klegg said to Alina, ushering her from her seat.

"Oh yes, yes!" Alina said. She waved to Gretchen. "I am so happy for you, *meine kleine schwester*. It brings me hope that my Werner will return to me!" She flounced from the room, curls bobbing and petticoats swishing.

"Tante Edelgard Klegg," Gretchen whispered, her temper flaring, "what have you done?"

EIGHT

Saturday, 15 April 1865 / Grove City, Ohio

Karl gnawed on the dried corn he found in the chicken coop. He figured the corn was worth getting his hands scratched by the aggressive chickens. His stomach gurgled, and the cow harmonized with it. Sitting with his legs outstretched, his toes knocked together. He cupped the small fistful of corn in his shirt and spit out a hard kernel butt.

He stared at the barn door, his jaw aching. Tante Klegg had been so swift to lock him in the barn again. Not that he could have stopped her. He could not stand without shaking.

Karl wondered if anyone "back home," wherever that was, missed him. It had been the norm in Camp Chase to have a woman waiting. All the prisoners whined and pined after their girls. The girls who got away, the girls who never made up their minds, and the girls waiting for their return.

Karl did not have those emotions, which he trusted more than his memory. He figured if he could not remember proposing, he would remember loving. No fresh, expectant face came to mind when he had lain in bed those long days and frigid nights last winter in prison.

Not that it mattered now. Whether someone waited for him or not, he now had a captor younger than he was. His captor's mother thought he had killed the president. His captor's aunt was equal parts mystic and militant. And they locked him in their barn.

Karl slowed his chewing, allowing his saliva to moisten the kernels. He studied the barn door, not sure what mechanism locked him inside and not sure when they would return. He sighed.

From one prison to another, this one was far more comfortable. At least here he could cuddle into the straw, scratchy though it was. A breeze whistled through a crack in the log wall, providing slight relief from the humidity. All in all, it was an improvement over the stuffy, fevered prison full of moans and dying and death.

"Don't know why I have to give him these," Gretchen said, sounding martyred just outside the door.

Karl straightened, upsetting the corn to the dirt floor. He brushed his hair back and rubbed his face with the hem of his shirt. Blast it if he was not going to try to look presentable.

Gretchen yanked the door open, almost right off its rusting hinges. "Here," she said, throwing clothes at him. "Put these on."

Karl studied the dark pants and white shirt in his lap. He could tell he would need to roll the pant hems. "Thank you."

"Thank my aunt," Gretchen said. She slumped against the door frame and crossed her arms. "She wants you to clean yourself and come to the house for supper."

"Why?" he asked.

Gretchen waved her hand, motioning she did not know and did not care. She disappeared, and for a moment Karl thought she left the door open for him to escape. She returned lugging a bucket of water with a ladle.

"I don't want to be here anymore than you want me here," Karl said. "But I got no place to go, and I can't keep going on what I got."

"You're staying," Gretchen said. She handed him a ladle of water and watched him guzzle it down. "And you're coming to eat dinner with us while we figure this out."

Karl rubbed the clothes in his hands. Gretchen had done a lot for him. She had brought him into her family home without approval from her aunt and mother. She had hid him from sight when danger arose.

"Whose clothes are these?" he asked.

"My brother's."

Karl wished he had not gulped the entire ladle of water. "Sorry. Which battle?"

Gretchen's expression soured. "My brother's coming back any day now. If you don't want clothes or food, then you can just sit here in the dark until we've decided what we're doing with you."

"No, wait. Don't leave me in the dark!" Karl cried as Gretchen swung open the barn door. He held his palm to his throbbing head and whimpered.

Gretchen stopped, her hand clenching the handle. "Someone knows you're here."

Karl rubbed his forehead. "Who?"

"Alina, the pastor's daughter."

"Why was the pastor's daughter at your house?"

"She's supposed to be my sister-in-law," Gretchen said through clenched teeth.

"Supposed to be?" Karl asked.

"When my brother returns, they'll marry." A breeze blew the skirt around Gretchen's ankles. "I don't know what you look like under all that dirt and blood. Use that water to wash up. There's a rag on a hook in the corner."

Karl glanced where she said the rag hung. "Near about killed myself trying to get this corn from the chickens. Would rather not tempt fate too many times in a day."

Gretchen stomped to the rag, snatched it from the hook, and threw it in Karl's lap with her brother's clothes. "I'll be outside." She slammed the door behind her.

Karl drank a good amount of the bucket. He let the water run down his neck, figuring he was not about to keep the clothes he was wearing, anyway. It was a wonder how clean the water felt, even in the dark. There were no maggots or twigs or any such debris to pick out. Just clean and wet. He rubbed the water onto his skin with a tender touch because bruises were everywhere. He peeled off his torn jacket and sour shirt, slathering the water up and down his arms and chest.

"Better wash that head wound," Gretchen called through the door. "Your temple's covered in blood. My mother won't eat if she has to stare at it."

Karl complied. He was unsure he got it all, but his head did feel less sticky. Fire ran from his shoulder to his fingertips when he tried to slip the cotton shirt over his head. He gasped through the pain.

"Doing all right in there?" Gretchen asked.

"Never you mind." He leaned back, panting from the exertion. "Don't you dare come in here. I ain't done yet." He tugged at his pant buttons and kicked them off so he could wash his feet.

"You're out of your head. Why would I come into the barn when you're naked?"

"I'm not naked," Karl grumbled. He yelped when the door opened. "I'm not dressed, either!"

"Well then, don't make it sound like you're ready!" Gretchen slammed the door shut again.

Soon enough, Karl had the pants on and rolled the hems so they did not drag beneath his feet. He knocked on the door.

"All right," he said when Gretchen opened it, "take me to your aunt."

NINE

Saturday, 15 April 1865 / Grove City, Ohio

"I cannot say what angers me more. That Alina was so excited about this criminal, or that she forgot Mr. Lincoln with such ease!" Gretchen's mother slammed a tin plate down on the table in front of Karl. He jumped, but otherwise kept his hands in his lap and was careful not to look anyone in the eye for too long.

Karl sat at the table in the kitchen with Tante Klegg beside him and Gretchen opposite him. The kitchen air was humid. The mouthwatering smells of roasted chicken and pickled onions chased his thoughts away.

"The child has to hold onto hope of Werner," Tante Klegg said.

"Our world is ending!" Gretchen's mother said, taking her seat and snatching her spoon. "The president has died at the hands of a Confederate! What will we have, four more years of war? Will my husband and son never return? All we've talked about is this waste of a man!" She gestured at Karl with a dismissive flick of her wrist.

Karl said nothing. Gretchen had warned him not to speak. Her mother was one bad piece of news away from harming herself or someone else. Karl poked at the onion in front of him, his appetite evaporating the longer Gretchen's mother spoke.

"But Mama," Gretchen said, "our world hasn't been as we knew it for years. It may never go back to the life we knew, especially if Werner and Papa don't return, or if they come back diff—"

Gretchen's mother slapped her so hard that Karl winced in sympathy. "Never," her mother said, "say those words. How you are a daughter of mine, I will never know."

Gretchen narrowed her eyes, trying to hide the tears lurking behind her lashes. She watched her mother turn her attention to her plate as if she had not struck her child.

Her mother ate her pickled onions with a slow grace that made Gretchen want to shove that spoon down her throat.

"His name is Karl, then?" Tante Klegg said, redirecting the conversation. She dipped her bread into the onion juice and took a healthy bite. "I thought he did not know his name? Perhaps you learned his name while undressing in his presence?"

"What are you talking about?" Gretchen's mother said, glaring at Tante Klegg. "What are you suggesting?"

Gretchen dropped her fork with a loud clatter. "I didn't—he didn't—he was out cold! You know that."

"You do not know that," Tante Klegg said. "You have compromised yourself, and our family name."

"I kicked him in the side, and he didn't even twitch. He didn't see anything. You didn't see anything!" Gretchen rounded on Karl, whose complexion dropped from a bright red to a sickly pale.

Karl rubbed his side. "Explains why my ribs hurt..."

"You're out of your mind," Gretchen said to Tante Klegg. "How can you think me changing in the barn is worse than keeping him captive until proven innocent? We won't know if he killed the president until he remembers."

"How can you compare this at all!" her mother scoffed.

"And?" Tante Klegg said, stabbing her chicken. "Has he remembered? Is his name Karl?"

"He... agreed his name was Karl when he woke," Gretchen replied.

"He agreed? You mean you gave him a name," Tante Klegg said. "You gave him the name of your grandfather. How could you?"

"There was blood at his temple. You saw it," Gretchen rushed to say. "He hurt his head and can't remember things. He agreed Karl was fine since he has no name."

Her mother snorted. "He thinks his name is Karl, he does not know his name. What else does he not know or remember?" She sawed the side of her fork into the overcooked chicken. "Killing the president? Fleeing the capital?"

"Would it make you feel better if I locked him up again?" Gretchen said.

Her mother rolled her eyes. "He is no danger to me right now, sitting here, this little weakling. It is only if someone sees him here with us. Tell me, Gretchen, Edelgard, why I have not run to the authorities to report this man yet."

Karl shrank in his seat.

"Because you would sentence us to prison with him," Tante Klegg said.

"For holding him hostage? We would be American heroes, not villains!"

Tante Klegg remained unconvinced.

"We cannot keep him long," Gretchen's mother warned. "The neighbors will wonder."

"Alina was happy to assume she knew the whole story," Tante Klegg said. "Others will do the same."

The sisters fell silent, their stormy expressions continuing the argument.

"Ma'am," Karl ventured, "I don't remember much of anything, if that's a comfort."

Gretchen's mother stared at him, her face changing colors while she struggled to find her words.

"You said he's my responsibility," Gretchen said. "What does it matter what his name is? I'm taking care of him."

"There are things you do not understand, *meine kleine trottel*," her mother said in saccharine tones.

Gretchen stiffened. Karl assumed it had something to do with her mother's condescending tone.

"We left Germany to avoid these political happenings," her mother continued. "Shooting leaders of nations! We left Europe because of such upheavals. America is not supposed to behave like this!"

"Mama, you are hysterical," Gretchen sighed.

She grabbed Gretchen by the jaw, her fingers pinching into Gretchen's cheeks. Gretchen whimpered as her mother jerked her forward so they were nose-to-nose.

"You listen to me," she said in a low, dangerous voice. "Who will be president now? Who? Johnson, who everyone hates? Seward, if he lives? This nation will fall, and you stand before me telling me I worry too much, that I should not care the enemy sleeps in my child's bedroom."

Tante Klegg put her hand out as if to separate them, but Gretchen's mother had already shoved her away. Gretchen fell back in her chair, rubbing her jaw and staring at her mother with wide, wary eyes.

"You and everyone in this country lived a blessed life before the war," her mother said, heaving from the table. "But we knew, your Tante Klegg and I. We left that behind. And now look, we live it again. There is no stopping human nature. What if he kills us in our sleep?"

"We're taking care of him," Gretchen protested. "He wouldn't kill us."

"Taking care of a man does not earn his loyalty. And if he has no idea of his past, it does not give you the right to take his identity from him!"

"What identity?" Tante Klegg said. "He said he remembers nothing."

Gretchen's mother closed her eyes and rubbed her temples. "What if he wakes up, and his name is not Karl, and he is the man who shot the president? Do you realize what you subject us to if we do not turn him in? This is treason!"

Gretchen gnawed on her bread. "What if he never remembers?" she asked around the bread remaining in her mouth.

"Do not speak with food in your mouth. What if he does remember?" Tante Klegg said.

Gretchen's chewing slowed. "If he remembers, then we'll have to see what he remembers. If he killed the president, we turn him in. If he didn't, we can't turn in an innocent man."

"He might be a fugitive from Camp Chase," Tante Klegg pointed out.

The woman was infuriating. "Tante Klegg, you're the one who told me to bring him in the house," Gretchen said.

Gretchen's mother began shouting in German. The way Tante Klegg frowned and Gretchen's mouth dropped open made Karl assume Gretchen's mother was swearing up a storm. When she finally stopped, everyone looked at each other, impressed.

Trying to downplay her mother's fury, Gretchen popped a thick slice of onion into her mouth. "He's too weak to escape, memories or not."

"Food, Gretchen," Tante Klegg ground out. "Chew it."

"We have no reason to keep him here," Gretchen's mother said, glowering at Karl. "He speaks and moves well enough. He should take his chances."

There was no way he would survive another night without shoes, or a hat, or some water. Karl settled his spoon beside his plate and stared at his lap. If this was how a bunch of women treated him, what would happen if he ran into a bunch of angry soldiers?

"And what are your thoughts on this?" Gretchen's mother demanded of Karl. "You would allow my daughter to ruin herself, attached to a criminal?"

"I'm not attached to him!" Gretchen said, exasperated.

"Gretchen, you would do well to shut your mouth before she grabs you again," Tante Klegg said.

"Don't know as I'd say I'm a criminal, ma'am," Karl said.

"You were in prison. You must have done something," Gretchen's mother pointed out.

Gretchen nibbled on her fingernail.

"Lots of men go to prison in war, ma'am, for lots of reasons," Karl said.

"Papa would be unhappy with us for quarreling this way, Mama," Gretchen said. "He believed in our president's goals for a unified nation."

Her mother scoffed. "He is our prisoner. He will do as we say until we are certain he did not shoot the president, and that the war will not start again." She leaned forward, pointing at Gretchen. "You play in a world you do not understand, *kleines mädchen*. But you will learn soon."

She took her plate of onions and boiled chicken with her as she left the room. She slammed her bedroom door. They heard the ropes creak as she plopped onto her bed.

"So I am to sleep in a bed smelling of onions," Tante Klegg said. Ever since Gretchen's father had left, Tante Klegg had taken to sharing a bed with her sister, leaving the attic to Gretchen.

Gretchen glanced at Karl and frowned. "What are we going to do with him?" she asked Tante Klegg. "We can't hide him forever."

Tante Klegg made a point of eating the rest of her meal before responding. Even though Gretchen fidgeted, she respected the silence. Karl, feeling his stomach churn now that Gretchen's mother had left the room, dug into his food.

"You remember when Mr. Lincoln came to Columbus," Gretchen said. "We read it in the papers. He wanted a united house. A house can't get more united than ours right now, a Reb with a bunch of Unionists. He's trying to get home, like Werner. Like Papa. Mama acts like I'm doing this to try to hurt her."

"You do not have to try to hurt your mother, but it happens anyway. That is the problem," Tante Klegg said and she patted her lips with her washing rag.

Gretchen leaned back in her chair, her expression the saddest thing Karlhad seen since leaving the prison.

"You will come to church with us tomorrow," Tante Klegg told Karl. "You will sit in our pew. You will act as if you sing our songs."

Gretchen cocked her head to the side. "Why would he do that?"

"Alina has seen him. She has told her father, we must assume this. Tomorrow is Easter, and we must go to church. Alina's father the pastor will question why we have not brought our poor soldier friend."

Gretchen pondered this. "But why should Karl have to pretend he knows our songs? "

"He must show an effort to learn our ways, or no one will believe he is your *verlobter*."

Gretchen hunched over her plate. "Oh, go on, pile on the agony. No one will believe we're engaged no matter what we do. Everybody knows I'm going to be a spinster."

Tante Klegg tapped her fork on the back of Gretchen's hand. "Perhaps that would have been true yesterday, but yesterday, you did not undress in the presence of a man."

"You can't make me marry this man. That's the rest of my life with a stranger! A stranger without memories!"

"What did you think was going to happen, bringing him in?" Tante Klegg asked.

"I thought... I thought we would give him time to heal, to make his way home." Gretchen scratched the back of her head, disturbing her braids. "I wanted to help him, hoping someone would help Papa." She looked out the window. "What if this doesn't work? What if his memories come back and he is a murderer?"

"Men disappear all the time," Tante Klegg said.

Gretchen blinked at her aunt, stunned.

"Do you understand me, Karl?" Tante Klegg asked. Her voice was gentle, and her gaze did not waver.

Karl looked up from his plate, his face red and his eyes sparking. "Yes, ma'am."

PRESIDENT ANDREW JOHNSON'S SPEECH

Sunday, 16 April 1865 / Washington City, District of Columbia

THE POLICY HE IS LIKELY TO PURSUE.

In this morning's Statesman we reproduce the speech of Andrew Johnson, now President of the United States, delivered by him on the 5th of April, at Washington City, on the reception of the news of the fall of Richmond. It will be seen that in this speech he took the position decidedly, that if the power were in his hands, he would arrest, try, convict, and hang the leaders of the Rebellion.

"Death to the conspirators" — "Death is too easy a punishment" — "for his that is willing to list his impious hand against the authority of the Nation" — "the halter to intelligent, influential traitors," were utterances to which he gave emphasis. He seemed to regard it a duty to mold public opinion in conformity with these views. They are the views that have found special favor in the eyes of radicals in his party.

In view of the great calamity that has befallen the country in the assassination of President Lincoln, it is not likely that President Johnson will be moved to adopt a more humane policy toward the Rebels...

TEN

***

Sunday, 16 April 1865 / Grove City, Ohio

Gretchen hid a yawn behind her gloved hand. She squeezed into place between Karl and Tante Klegg on the church pew. While Tante Klegg had tended to the cow and chickens that morning, Gretchen had fashioned their mourning accessories for church. Karl wore a black armband while Gretchen, her aunt, and mother tacked black ribbons to their bonnets. Gretchen wove the extra black ribbons in her hair, which she wore up. She could not remember the last time she had felt so tired or had seen the church so packed.

No, that was not true. Every Easter the congregation size swelled, only to trickle down again by the next week. Even so, the church was filled to bursting, no doubt because of Mr. Lincoln's death.

Gretchen yawned again.

Pastor Baumbach frowned at Gretchen from the pulpit. He was tall, with a respectable beard and healthy belly. He spoke to the congregation, a brow raised in disapproval.

"This is a time for reflection and prayer now more than ever," Pastor Baumbach said in his thick accent. This was his second meeting of the day. Usually, the German sermon happened on the week opposite of the English sermons. Today, the German sermon had preceded the English one, and everyone remained. There was hardly space for Gretchen's family when they had arrived.

"It was only Friday when we celebrated the end of this terrible war and a Good Friday it was," Pastor Baumbach said. "Yesterday, we heard of the great Republican martyr. Today, we mourn the loss of a great man and leader, the only soul who knew how best to heal this scarred country. Mr. Lincoln proclaimed freedom, and there was freedom! He led this sinning nation to the promised land. Yet, like Moses, he was not permitted to see the fruits of this promised land himself."

Pastor Baumbach turned from Gretchen finally, and she released a breath she did not know she held.

"We know not what sort of evil condoned and conspired to carry out these terrible actions. But we all have seen how war changes a man." Pastor Baumbach nodded to a returned soldier who sat in the front pew with slumped shoulders and one leg. "All we can do now is pray. Pray for our sacrificed leader, pray for all the dark souls involved in this crime. Encourage each other to turn to Christ for hope in this dark time. Watch for your families as they return home from battle. May we never see a war the like of this ever again."

Pastor Baumbach sighed at his congregation and continued with regular worship.

Gretchen's nostrils flared while hiding yet another yawn during the singing. Tante Klegg elbowed her. Gretchen grabbed the pew in front of her to keep from tumbling into Karl. Her fingers scratched the shoulder of the elderly woman in front of her, who turned to scowl.

Gretchen smiled her apology and released the pew. She rubbed her side, her expression mulish when she glanced at Tante Klegg.

Karl shivered beside Gretchen, and she saw great drops slide down his face and neck.

They sat for the sermon when the music concluded. Karl frowned the entire time until they stood again to leave the little wood frame church. Gretchen pushed Karl so he stepped into the aisle. She knelt to genuflect to the front of the church, mimicking her mother and aunt.

When Gretchen stood and looped her hand through Karl's arm, he swayed. He waited for her to lead the way.

"*Fräulein* Miller, you must introduce your friend," Pastor Baumbach said to Gretchen.

Karl froze. Gretchen let her hand slip a little, trying to step away from him, but Tante Klegg nudged them both closer to the door.

"Remember," Tante Klegg whispered behind them, "you mustered out at Camp Chase. You are returning home to Ironton."

Gretchen gulped as they inched closer, feeling sweat dripping down her back. She was not ready to lie to her pastor, though she often lied to Alina to pass the time.

Pastor Baumbach knew Gretchen's every sin, since her mother delighted in telling him. And besides, Gretchen had admitted enough of her faults over the years. That she harbored a Confederate who could be Mr. Lincoln's murderer was difficult. Lying about it to Pastor Baumbach's face seemed to put Gretchen's soul at even more risk.

Alina's squeal bounced into the conversation from behind the pastor. "Oh Papa, you do not know? This is Gretchen's *verlobter!*" Alina jumped into view. Her wide skirts swung as she dragged her mother by the arm up the few stairs to meet them in the doorway.

Gretchen pressed her lips together as everyone stared at her. Someone whispered they never thought the Miller girl would find herself a husband.

Pastor Baumbach's eye twinkled in the glinting sunlight. He ran his hand down his short beard and asked, "Is this so, Gretchen?"

Gretchen dropped Karl's arm and refused to step forward despite Tante Klegg poking her. Where would Alina have come up with such an idea? They had said no such thing yesterday before she left. Gretchen turned to swat at Tante Klegg and caught sight of her mother's little smile. Gretchen's stomach dropped, and her mind raced.

There could be no reason why her mother would say such a thing to Alina. Her mother wanted Karl out of the house as much as she wanted Papa and Werner back in it. Telling Alina that Karl and Gretchen were engaged would keep him around longer!

Then again, if Gretchen went along with Alina's nonsense, it would be a great distraction while they helped Karl remember who he was. Arranged marriages were not that out of the ordinary, especially among German families. Other women married to take care of family farms while their fathers and brothers left for war. Some women even seemed to like their husbands.

Karl could have been someone Gretchen's father selected before leaving for war. It could have happened.

Tante Klegg chuckled, which made Gretchen's hair stand on end. "Dear Alina, so determined to marry off everyone."

Alina reddened and straightened an invisible wrinkle in her skirts.

Pastor Baumbach studied Gretchen. "I have not seen him before, Gretchen. This is sudden." He rubbed his beard. "But then, war forces us to make sudden decisions."

Gretchen understood his undertone. He wanted to hear her say that this stranger meant something to her.

"This man is like Werner," Gretchen said. "He is an injured soldier looking for home."

Pastor Baumbach nodded. He noted the bandage around Karl's head and the sweat beading at Karl's temples.

"It is clear he is too ill to fight," Tante Klegg chimed in, moving to grab Karl's arm before his knees buckled.

"He is ill?" Pastor Baumbach asked, drawing a handkerchief from his sleeve to cover his mouth.

Tante Klegg shook her head. "He suffers from terrors, waking and sleeping. He does not know who he is. He does not know where he is. We brought him to church for healing of his mind."

Gretchen stared at Tante Klegg. Her falsehoods were so smooth that even Gretchen believed them.

Pastor Baumbach reached forward to pat Karl on the shoulder, but Karl jumped back. "Do not worry, child. I mean only to give you blessings."

"Reckon I'll feel blessed enough from here, thank you," Karl said.

Pastor Baumbach frowned. "Where did you say he was from?" he asked Gretchen's mother.

"I did not say." She picked up her skirts and inched around the small party.

"Do you approve of these doings?" Pastor Baumbach said to Tante Klegg once Gretchen's mother left the church. "She is a child."

"I'm fifteen," Gretchen said.

"This is why we wait for her father," Tante Klegg said in a sweet tone. "Her mother worries she is not ready, but I have seen her run the farm as her father would have wished. Gretchen is ready for more responsibility."

Gretchen glanced at Karl. More responsibility sounded like adding another chore, not caring for a strange man in a strange land during strange times.

Karl was rigid, hands clenched at his sides. Sweat pooled under his arms and on his chest, and he vibrated with tension.

"He doesn't know where he's from," Tante Klegg said, wrenching Gretchen out of her thoughts. "His head won't let him remember."

Pastor Baumbach's mouth twisted.

"It's like you said in the sermon," Gretchen rushed, "we're encouraging him to hope. It must be so scary to not know where you're from." She took Karl's arm and inched around Pastor Baumbach and Alina. "I'm sure when he feels better we will have you over to visit. When Papa returns."

"Gretchen!" Pastor Baumbach said, stopping Gretchen and Karl a few feet from the church door. "You must be careful in these dark days. We do not know who we can trust."

Gretchen nodded and scurried away, dragging Karl with her. "We'll need to figure you out sooner than we thought," she said when they reached the wagon. She hitched her skirts, about to hike up onto the wagon seat to drive the horses back to the farm.

On second thought, she turned to shout, "Coming, Alina?"

ELEVEN

Sunday, 16 April 1865 / Grove City, Ohio

"Poor creature," Alina crooned, dragging her fingers across Karl's hand. They sat close together. Alina had not stopped touching Karl since entering the house.

Karl looked much better now that Tante Klegg had given him a bowl of stew.

"To not know who you are," Alina said, shaking her head, "or where you are! It was so good of Gretchen and her *tante* and *mütter* to take you in, so good!"

Gretchen squirmed when Alina glared at her.

"Almost too good," Alina said.

Tante Klegg, who stirred the evening stew, straightened but did not turn around.

"It must be so nice to be among friends again," Alina said.

Karl nodded. He was careful not to look at Gretchen. He did not want to make it obvious that he had no idea what he should say.

Alina squinted at him. "Do you remember who told you to come to this house?"

"We said he doesn't know who he is," Gretchen said. "How could he remember who told him to come here?"

Karl raised his hand to silence Gretchen. "I can speak for myself, thanks."

That made Tante Klegg whip around, dripping ladle in hand. Her brow quirked.

Gretchen shrugged as if to say, "Fine, it's your hanging."

"I'm mighty thankful for your interest, Miss..." Karl waited for Alina to supply her name. "Miss Alina. Well, ain't that a pretty name. Does it have a meaning? Seems like it should. I don't know if I've ever heard a name like that. But then, I don't have my right mind so it could be that I have. Don't remember either way."

Alina flushed and dropped Karl's hand so that she could untie her bonnet strings.

Gretchen and Tante Klegg stared at Karl as if he had grown horns and pustules on his face. They did not dare look at one another, not with Alina distracted.

"Right glad you're sitting there, Miss Alina," Karl continued. "You see, the light from that window there hits your hair and makes it shine a bit. What would you call your hair?"

"My *mütter* calls it corn yellow," Alina said to her lap, her ears red.

"Corn yellow?" Karl scoffed. "What a thing for a mother to say. Why, it's a sunflower sort of yellow. Have you ever seen a sunflower? They rejoice under sunlight, reaching to the sky, to God. Boasting their love of life so tall that no one can avoid seeing them."

Gretchen did not understand this change in Karl. Was it only yesterday he cowered in her brother's bed, eyes so wide, voice so frail? This Karl kept his voice low, pleasing, and deferential. He was confident. He knew how to distract pretty girls.

It was all Gretchen could do to stand there and watch Alina eat Karl's words like dessert. Gretchen could not leave; she had to make sure Karl did not betray them. But she also could not stay, not with things going the way they were.

Alina looked up, entranced. "Sunflowers sound beautiful," she said. Her voice was so full of yearning it begged Karl to complete the compliment and call her beautiful, too.

"Do you think Werner has seen any sunflowers?" Gretchen said.

Alina jumped in her seat and turned around, having forgotten anyone else was in the small kitchen. Karl glared at Gretchen.

"I hope so," Alina said, now wistful. "Werner loved my hair. I hope sunflowers make him feel closer to me." She rummaged in her little fringed purse for a handkerchief. "I have nothing to make me feel closer to him."

"Nonsense," Gretchen said. "You have us, don't you? Isn't that why you come every day?"

Alina sniffled behind her handkerchief. "I come to tell you the news, because you are so far from town. You have no idea what is happening in the search for the president's killer, do you?"

Gretchen wished she had kept her mouth shut.

"What are they saying?" Tante Klegg asked. Her stern expression dared Karl or Gretchen to breathe a word and see the consequences.

Alina clenched her hands in her lap. "You were not at the capital yesterday. My parents and I, we rushed to Columbus to hear the latest after I left this house. It takes so long for the news to come to Grove City," she said in an aside to Karl. "We could not wait after we heard what happened."

Gretchen rolled her eyes.

"They wound black fabric around the capital building's columns," Alina said. "Everyone spoke in hushed voices. We were all so shocked, so sad. Flags were so low on their poles, they almost touched the ground. There were military companies from the Tod Barracks and Camp Chase, too."

Karl stiffened at the mention of Camp Chase.

Alina described the masses of people wandering Columbus. Businesses closed every minute as the news spread of the president's death. Columbus was usually a place of grand adventure, so many people, so many shops! But not on Saturday, not on the afternoon of the president's death.

"To think," Alina said, shaking her head, "we won the war, to have our president killed like this." She slapped the table, startling everyone in the room. "I hope to God that Werner killed every last one he saw. Those dirty, terrible rascals!"

Karl glanced at Gretchen. A bead of sweat appeared at his temple, which should not have comforted Gretchen, but it did.

"These are hard times," Tante Klegg said. "We hate the Confederates for splitting away. They hate us for forcing them to stay."

Everyone stared at her.

"Tante Klegg," Alina said, "you sound... sympathetic!"

"I have been through a war before, child, you forget that. It is never as simple as the papers will make you believe." Tante Klegg turned when the stew popped behind her. "Now, you must tell me why you told your papa that Gretchen was engaged to Karl."

Gretchen grabbed the chair opposite Karl and plopped into it. "Yes, Linnie," she said, using Werner's pet name for Alina, "tell us."

"Wait," Karl said, holding up his hands. "I thought y'all was joking."

"That's what 'verlobter,' means," Gretchen said. "It means we're courting."

Karl ran his finger along his collar. "Ain't that something."

Ears redder than before, Alina dabbed her handkerchief at her temple. "You must not think me wicked."

"Why shouldn't I?" Gretchen said before she could help it. She rested her elbows on the table, even though she knew she would get a slap from Tante Klegg.

Alina pulled out a careworn piece of paper from her purse. She placed it on the table and would not remove her hand from it. "I received a letter from Werner."

Tante Klegg dropped the ladle on the floor and glanced at her sister's bedroom.

Gretchen jumped. "And you kept it from us?"

"I'm sharing with you now," Alina said, as if to a child.

"Alina," Gretchen said, "that letter is fraying. How long have you had a letter from my brother?"

"It wasn't a letter for his sister, it was a letter for his love," Alina shot back. "And I'm sharing it with you, now that you also have happy news, now that you have a *verlobter*!"

"You should have shared the letter anyway!" Gretchen said.

Tante Klegg hissed from the stove, "Lower your voice while your mother sleeps! How will she react to knowing there was a letter from her son and she did not know it?"

Gretchen and Alina looked at each other and sat down.

Karl broke the heavy silence. "What does it say?"

"I thought you would be happy to know he lives," Alina whispered. Tears gathered in her eyes. "I thought this would make *Mütter* happy."

"Please do not share the parts specific about your love," Gretchen said. "I have to eat Tante Klegg's stew later."

That remark earned a soupy slap on the back of her neck from Tante Klegg, but Gretchen did not care. There was a letter from Werner, which meant he was alive. Or he had been alive whenever Alina received the letter. Or he had been alive in the weeks before Alina received the letter.

There were still battles in Tennessee despite the ceasefire. And there was no knowing where Werner's regiment sneaked to these days.

"It's short," Alina admitted. "I was unsure it was Werner's hand, at first. He said he's glad to come home soon, that he couldn't wait to settle, to forget the horrors he had seen. He wants a family of his own."

"What's wrong with the one he has now?" Gretchen said.

"You remember those days before he left for the war," Alina said. "He itched under your papa's command to stay home and take care of you, your mother, your aunt. How many times he cried into my lap, saying he wanted to defend his country! And you were all so angry with him when he finally left!"

Gretchen stared at Alina, dumbfounded. That was not the brother Gretchen remembered. Crying into a girl's skirt? Angry with their father? Werner seemed so calm in the days before he ran away.

"He wants to be a father," Alina continued, her face aflame. "And he wants to see you happy and married, too, Gretchen."

Karl leaned forward. "So when you learned about me, you thought I was the perfect fit, and it was time to let them know Werner was returning."

Alina nodded, too embarrassed to look him in the eye. "But, your accent..."

Karl leaned back. "What about my accent?"

Alina paused, unsure how to continue. "It would be so good if you could remember who you were in time for Werner's return. If we knew... You sound so southern."

"He thinks his family is from Ironton," Gretchen said, perpetuating Tant Klegg's lies.

"Wonderful!" Alina clapped her hands. "We could have a double wedding! My papa would be happy to do it!"

Gretchen and Karl looked in opposite directions, mortified.

"If not for each other, for Werner?" Alina said. "His letter says he could arrive any day."

Everyone jumped when Gretchen's mother slammed her bedroom door open. "Werner?" she screamed. "My Werner returns?"

TWELVE

Sunday, 16 April 1865 / Grove City, Ohio

Gretchen rolled her eyes at Alina, who dangled the letter from her fingers. Alina stared at Gretchen's mother, horrified.

"You *had* to raise your voice," Gretchen said.

Karl half-stood, gripping the back of his chair to stop the room from spinning. "Think I should head on back to the barn?"

Tante Klegg pointed at the chair with her dripping ladle. "Sit."

Karl sank. "Don't see how my face will help anything."

Gretchen's mother shoved her out of the way. "What do you know of Werner?"

Gretchen caught herself on the table corner. "Have a nice nap, Mama?" she said.

Tante Klegg clapped her hand on Gretchen's shoulder and shook her head. Gretchen shrugged.

Alina flourished the letter. "Werner returns!" She scurried around the table, her skirts swishing as she reached for Gretchen's mother. "He wrote, and I waited for the right time to tell you…"

Gretchen's mother expression hardened as she backed away from Alina. "Do you believe I would let my son marry a girl like you?"

Alina's smile faltered. "*Mütter?*"

Gretchen's mother pointed at Alina, but spoke to Tante Klegg. "You have seen this letter?"

Tante Klegg shook her head. "The child showed me nothing. She keeps it in her hand."

Alina inched behind Karl, who remained frozen in place. She pressed the letter into Tante Klegg's hands, now afraid to approach Gretchen's mother.

Tante Klegg looked at her sister, at Gretchen, and down at the fragile paper in her hands. "It looks like his handwriting."

Gretchen's mother snatched the letter from Tante Klegg. She read it, her lips moving as she brought it closer to her face until she stood there smelling the paper in silence.

"He's coming home to us, *Mütter*," she whispered.

Before anyone could stop her, Gretchen's mother ripped the letter into shreds.

Alina fell to her knees to gather the pieces. She scooped them into her lap, her skirt puffing around her as she sat in the dust. "I wanted to wait until I was sure," she cried. "Now that the war is over, I knew Werner would come home soon. I wanted to make you happy."

"You thought you would be my hero?" Gretchen's mother's voice was soft and cold, far more frightening than her usual hysterics. "My hero is my son coming home to me. My hero is my husband bringing my son home from war. My hero is bringing my life back to order. You are a manipulative child."

Alina sobbed, shaking her head and pressing the letter pieces to her heart.

Gretchen scratched her eyebrow with a grimace. If anyone were to make a letter the subject of dramatics, it would be her mother and Alina. Not that she was in any place to judge. She was furious with Alina for hiding the letter. Watching Alina cry made Gretchen happier than she had felt in a while. The fact that her mother brought Alina to tears only made it better.

Tante Klegg moved the pot of stew off the burner. The scraping noise startled everyone. "Your son has written to say he returns," she said. "Why are you upset?"

"You know why," Gretchen's mother said. "Why did he not write me?"

"You do not know he did not," Tante Klegg pointed out. "The post is unreliable. We should be glad we know anything about Werner."

Gretchen's mother crossed her arms over her chest. "You cannot believe that."

"What is there to believe these days?" Tante Klegg said with a shrug. "We live in the days of men shooting presidents. What I believe does not matter."

Gretchen's mother leaned over the table. "This is exactly when what you believe does matter."

Tante Klegg inhaled as if struck.

Gretchen flinched, waiting for another outburst. Next thing she knew, her mother was in her bedroom again. No one followed her.

Karl heaved a sigh and slouched. Tante Klegg huffed and turned back to the stove, clanging her spoon as she stirred.

"So we discovered what it takes for my mother to turn on you," Gretchen said to Alina.

Alina stared at Gretchen, eyes narrowing.

"Good luck getting on her good side again," Gretchen continued. "I've been trying since I was born."

Alina smiled, rested her hands on her hips, and said, "Don't you ever get tired of being ignored?"

"What?" Gretchen said.

"I was trying to help you," Alina said. "Nothing makes a young woman more important than her wedding. She means something if she's a wife. Don't you pay attention in church? This would have been the making of you!"

"I pay plenty of attention," Gretchen said, "and I don't need your help. My papa told me everyone means something in this world, and I don't have to get married to mean something."

Alina snorted. "Your papa was a lazy man. He pretended he was a philosopher. He fooled no one. He was an Ohio farmer who married the daughter of a German intellectual. Or so she claims."

Gretchen's fist landed on Alina's jaw before she gave it much thought. Alina fell back, screaming, using both hands to hold her face together.

Karl leaped from his seat to catch Alina. Tante Klegg wrapped her arm around Gretchen's shoulders.

"Try to marry my brother after saying a thing like that," Gretchen said. She panted, struggling against Tante Klegg's grip. "I dare you."

Karl righted Alina. She let him check her jaw and smirked at Gretchen even though tears ran down her face.

Gretchen lunged. Tante Klegg threw her against the wall.

"Compose yourself," Tante Klegg said. "You—what's your name—Karl, escort Alina out."

"How am I supposed to get home? You made me ride with you!" Alina whined.

"It is broad daylight, girl," Tante Klegg said. "Walk."

Alina swished her skirts and held out her hand in a way that implied she expected Karl to offer his arm. He did, but with a little frown as Alina led him to the porch. Every step echoed on the puncheon floor, inflaming Gretchen's anger.

"Let me loose," Gretchen said. She met Tante Klegg's glare from the corner of her eye. "Are you going to take her side after the way she spoke about Werner?"

"You attacked Werner's betrothed," Tante Klegg said, releasing Gretchen. "She is his choice. If this ever gets back to him, what do you think he will do to you?"

Gretchen's mind flashed back to when Werner had tied her to a post in the back of the chicken coop. It had taken her hours to loosen the knots. Everyone had blamed her for upsetting the chickens, which refused to lay eggs for weeks after that. All because Gretchen had said Werner's hair looked silly all done up with pomade.

"You are so rash, Gretchen," Tante Klegg sighed. She rubbed her hands down her face, muttering that Gretchen was too like her mother.

Gretchen's face inflamed. She might be rash, but she was not hysterical or silly. "I am nothing like her," she said, surprising Tante Klegg. "When Papa and Werner left, she cried for weeks. They left me with the revolver. They left me to look after you and Mama."

Tante Klegg's smile was wry. "And you did not think, not once, that your papa might have asked someone to look after you?"

Gretchen blinked. No, that had not occurred to her. It had never occurred to her that her father would ask her aunt to watch after her, rather than her own mother. She looked at her mother's bedroom door, which muffled her mother's sobs. Her face crumpled. Did her mother hate her so much that even her father did not trust Gretchen to her care?

Tante Klegg patted Gretchen's cheek. "Do not let your Karl leave the room before I return." She left the kitchen as Karl entered it.

"You all right?" he asked, finding Gretchen staring at her hands.

Gretchen shrugged. "As all right as a person who's no good for anything could be." She watched the sunset blaze through the kitchen window, shielding her gaze. "Day's almost done. We'll have to figure out where to put you for the night." Gretchen squinted at him. "You seem to be feeling better. You walked Alina all the way to the barn and back by yourself?"

"Food and water does wonders," Karl said.

"You hardly ate anything," Gretchen said.

"Saw a man come out of a fever in the prison, and he ate so much so fast he had pains for days and died anyway. I'm fine with taking my time."

"Obviously," Gretchen said, crossing her arms over her chest.

Karl scoffed. "Tell me you're not jealous."

"Of course not! I'm worried. Alina's got her own agenda with you, and I don't understand it. We've got to get you well enough to get out of here before anyone realizes we're not engaged."

Tante Klegg reappeared with rope in her hand. She gestured at an empty chair. "I will take the legs."

"What?" Karl and Gretchen said in unison.

Tante Klegg clicked her tongue against the top of her mouth. "We will tie him to the chair. I will take the legs. You will lift from behind."

"I'm not doing this," Gretchen said. "He won't be any trouble. We can lock him in the barn. Or he can sleep in the hayloft."

Tante Klegg motioned for Karl to sit in the chair.

Karl studied the chair, considering his options. The chair seat was smooth from years of family meals. It was more comfortable than the rough boards he used to sleep on in the prison. Sure, it would be less comfortable sitting upright all night. But there would not be wind whistling through large gaps in the walls. And it was still better than his imprisoned nights at Camp Chase.

Karl figured no one would kill him in the kitchen, even though they liked waving their revolver around. He sat down.

Tante Klegg grunted as she wound the rope around Karl's ankles, lashing them to the chair legs. She led the rope up, over his lap, and around his wrists. She wrapped it under his armpits and over his shoulders to the back of the chair.

"Where did you learn to do that?" Gretchen said.

"Lift and shut your mouth," Tante Klegg said.

Karl stiffened with a gasp when he was airborne. His fingers gripped the edges of his seat to stabilize, not that it helped. Ropes strained across his sunken chest, wound around his waist, and spiraled down his legs. They did not cushion Gretchen and Tante Klegg's jarring missteps across the kitchen.

Karl could not help it. He whimpered as they reached Werner's room.

"It's not any fun down here, either," Gretchen grunted between clenched teeth.

"This is the consequence of your impetuousness," Tante Klegg said. She stumbled, and Karl tipped forward, his knees slamming into her shoulders. "Gretchen, hold onto him!"

Gretchen dropped the back legs so Karl and the chair were safe on the ground. "Let's leave him out here," she suggested, panting. "He won't be comfortable anywhere we put him if he's stuck in that chair."

"Y'all could let me loose," Karl suggested.

Tante Klegg grabbed the back of the chair and began to drag him. "My sister is not a terrible shot," she grunted. "Do you think she will forget your unfortunate allegiance because of Alina's betrayal?"

That was a good point. Gretchen helped push Karl into Werner's bedroom. Maybe she was good for nothing. But at least she could help Karl stay alive another night.

THIRTEEN

Monday, 17 April 1865 / Grove City, Ohio

Karl's head rung so hard he could not keep his eyes open. He cupped his hands over his ears and fell with his head bowed and his knees hugged to his chest. He whispered prayers to himself, hoping it would all be over soon. Screams erupted around him, man and animal. He looked up to find large sausages spilling from what had been a fine thoroughbred.

He watched, horrified, at the steam rising from the disemboweled horse. Karl's stomach rebelled. He retched up the wormy hardtack he had choked down that morning. When there was nothing left to retch, he joined in the screams that surrounded him. He screamed until he was guttural. He screamed past having a voice.

He was not supposed to be here.

"Wake up!"

A hand shook Karl hard. His head slammed into a wall, or headboard, or something upright and wooden.

"Are you trying to wake the entire county?" Tante Klegg said.

Karl squinted, his head throbbing. Through a fog, he realized he was not caught in a battle. He tried wiping the sweat from his forehead, but could not move his hand. Panicking, he rocked from side to side.

Tante Klegg loomed over him in the darkness. Her white nightdress pooled at her feet. She had thrown a knitted shawl over her shoulders. "Are you done?" she asked.

"I told you we shouldn't have tied him up," Gretchen said from behind Tante Klegg. She shuffled closer, barefoot. One hand held her cotton shift off the floor; the other clutched a dripping candle.

Tante Klegg shrugged in the dim, flickering light.

Karl blinked a burning bead of sweat from his eye. "Y'all have a bad habit of creeping up on a person." The tremor in his voice marred his attempt at bravado.

"You're drenched," Gretchen said.

He was, right through Werner's shirt. Gretchen's mother would be unhappy when she found out.

As if hearing his thoughts, Gretchen glanced at the empty trunk at the end of Werner's bed. "We only have that one set of clothes from Werner. We don't have anything else to change you into."

"Do you want to tell us why you screamed?" Tante Klegg asked, pulling the candle from Gretchen.

Karl shook his head, not wanting to relive his nightmare. Bile rose in his throat, and sweat streamed down his back. He did not understand why Tante Klegg and Gretchen wore shawls with their nightgowns. There he sat, sodden with sweat, and they shivered in the nighttime air.

Tante Klegg turned away, taking the candle with her.

"Please don't take the light away," Karl whispered.

"Tell us what made you scream," she said. Her voice was quiet, calm, and demanding.

"We should let him rest, he's feverish again," Gretchen said after brushing the wet hair from his forehead.

Tante Klegg glared at Gretchen, looking even more ominous in the faltering light. "The boy needs to remember who he is. He has no time for being coddled now that Pastor Baumbach thinks you are to marry him."

"But he's—"

"Gretchen!" Tante Klegg said. She moved for the door, the room darkening with each step.

Karl's breath quickened. His shoulders tensed. His stomach flipped. It was too dark. The dark smothered him. Karl closed his eyes and saw a flash of the disemboweled horse. He cried out. "Horses," he said, "torn to pieces right in front of me. Could've been me!"

Tante Klegg turned around, and the light shone in Karl's eyes. "What else?"

He stared into the candle's firelight until spots danced. Karl shook his head. He could say no more. Nothing would stop the nightmares now. Karl and the other prisoners—they had realized that in Camp Chase. A man could talk until he lacked a voice. Nothing stopped the nightmares or waking dreams.

Gretchen gathered her nightgown and knelt beside him. "Was the war that bad?" Some emotion that Karl could not place shone in her eyes. He almost thought it was concern for him. He was quick to remember he was nothing more than a stand-in for her brother.

"Don't think I lost my memory because the war was so great," Karl said. The ropes bit into his wrists and ankles.

Gretchen scowled. "Well, there's no cause to get feisty with me. I'm trying to be nice."

"Nice?" Karl echoed. "By giving me a name that don't belong to me?" If he had the ability, he might have thrown the chair across the room. Instead, he ground the ropes tighter into his skin as he fought against them.

Gretchen scrambled away, tripping over herself as she avoided Karl's thrashing.

"Forcing me to be your betrothed in daylight and tying me to a chair at night?" Karl laughed. "How's a man to remember a lifetime under these conditions?"

"Would you rather we left you to rot in our barn?" Gretchen asked.

Karl stared at Gretchen, whose expression was earnest and indignant. She was actually insulted. The girl had no idea what she was doing, like her aunt and mother kept telling her. "First off, that barn's the best thing that's happened to me since joining the war. A roof over my head and real straw to sleep on? A man could do a mite worse."

Gretchen sputtered.

"Do you think you're being charitable? I left that prison knowing if I didn't make that train, I'd be a dead man. And maybe I already am. Your brother's returning. He killed people like me. You think since the war's over he's going to welcome me? I'm the enemy, Gretchen!"

"You don't know that," Gretchen said. "You could be a good man still, if you wanted, and Werner wouldn't hurt you."

Karl shook his head. "Being a Confederate didn't make me a bad man. It just meant I believed something different than you."

The room fell silent.

"Gretchen," Tante Klegg said, still hovering by the doorway.

Gretchen stood. "That something different you believed in? It kept humans enslaved, beaten, and killed for generations. We aren't Quakers, but even we see that's wrong. And if that doesn't make you a bad man for believing in… that *peculiar institution*, then I don't know what does."

Karl's mouth hung open. "Peculiar institution." She said it was such disdain. That was the code word for slavery; he had learned it in the prison. He could not remember owning any slaves. He had no idea if all Confederate soldiers had slaves back home. It could be a Yankee legend about the rebels for all he knew.

"You missed a train?" Tante Klegg said.

"What?" Karl said, startled.

"You said you left the prison, and you missed a train." Tante Klegg rubbed her collarbone. "You did not escape?"

Karl stared at her. "I didn't escape?" he echoed.

"Escaped prisoners don't take the train," Tante Klegg said.

"General Morgan did," Gretchen said. She touched Tante Klegg's arm. "The newspapers said he walked right out of the penitentiary. That he took a train from Columbus to Cincinnati. How could you forget that? It was the only thing we talked about for months."

Tante Klegg jerked her arm away from Gretchen. The candle flickered, threatening to go out. "That was two years ago. Have you heard of anyone else escaping? There is a reason the cemetery is so full."

Karl shuddered. The Camp Chase cemetery was full; that was true. Last winter had been frigid. There had been little to protect the prisoners or staff from the smallpox outbreak. Karl pushed away memories of a bedmate carried to the pest house, never to return. Karl would never know why he was not moved to the pest house. He should have been. He should have died. He shared that bed with three men who died of the pox.

All Karl knew was what that nurse told him, the one who said he had to go on the train. Karl had been so malnourished that not even the pestilence had any interest in his skinny body.

Tante Klegg pointed at Karl, capturing his attention. "I am telling you, this boy is not a soldier. Even if he was, he is not anymore. And I do not think he escaped that prison. They let him go."

"That was a mistake we will not repeat, yes, Edelgarde?" Gretchen's mother said from the hallway. Her voice was soft. Gretchen and Tante Klegg whirled around.

"What are you doing?" Tante Klegg demanded.

Karl straightened in his seat. Something about Tante Klegg's voice made the hair on his arm stand on end. He peered around Tante Klegg and found Gretchen's revolver pointing at him. He hid behind Tante Klegg.

"Mama, where did you get that?" Gretchen asked. "That isn't yours to use."

"It was Werner's," her mother said in that soft voice. "I will use it in his honor, and with his permission."

"Mama," Gretchen warned, "you should go back to bed. We're handling this."

"Yes, I could hear you handling it with my door shut," she sneered. "The entire country heard you handling it. We are all traitors with him in our house, and you let him scream to the high heavens?"

"Stop talking to me as if I'm a child." Gretchen clenched her hands. "I know what we risk keeping Karl. It's what I hope some girl in the Confederacy is risking for Werner."

"His name is not Karl," her mother said. "He is not a good German boy. He is a dirty rebel. He is killing us by staying here."

"He is feverish and bound," Tante Klegg said. "No one would think him a guest in our house." She paused. "Gretchen's intentions were good, don't you think? The hopeful actions of a good... sister?"

"But where is Werner?" Gretchen's mother said. "He is lost to me. Lost..."

"Not according to Alina," Gretchen said. She nudged her aunt.

Tante Klegg's brows rose, and she stepped closer to her sister.

"That brat," Gretchen's mother snarled. "Hiding Werner's letter from us. Mark my words—she will not set foot in this house unless Werner himself forces me to make peace with her." Her hand slumped and the revolver dangled from her fingers.

Tante Klegg handed the candle to Gretchen. She took the revolver from her sister and wrapped an arm around her heaving shoulders.

"Keep watch over him," Tante Klegg instructed Gretchen. She led her sister to the kitchen and back to her bedroom. "If he screams, you will listen for clues and wake him if it is nonsense. You will learn who he is."

Gretchen protested, but fell back when Tante Klegg pointed the revolver at her.

"I am not in the habit of shooting children. This is no longer a lark, Gretchen. You will do as I say."

Gretchen held her hands high as she backed into Werner's bedroom.

"Think she'd shoot you?" Karl said in the dark after Tante Klegg shut the door.

"Your guess is as good as mine," Gretchen said. She crawled into Werner's bed and pulled the thin blanket atop her head. "Best get some sleep. We have chores in the morning. Know how to milk a cow?"

Karl shuddered. That cow was another lady waiting to have words with him. He closed his eyes and hoped he would have no more dreams that night.

FOURTEEN

_____

Monday, 17 April 1865 / Grove City, Ohio

Karl picked at a straw, ripping one thread off its length while Gretchen milked the cow. Her rhythmic pulls shot streams into the pail. "Milk seems thin."

"We keep a tight rein on her. People were having their livestock stolen, and we can't afford feed anymore. She eats the grass around the barn since that's all she can get to."

Karl nodded. That explained why the barn yard was barren, while the grass near the house was green.

The sound of the milk pulls was soothing in its repetition. Karl found himself wanting to doze the morning away. They had been in the barn since daybreak. Tante Klegg had ordered Karl to follow Gretchen during her morning chores. It turned out her chores happened to be caring for all the animals and the garden. In other words, her chores were everything on the farm. It seemed to Karl that Gretchen had to do everything that kept her out of the house.

"Does your mother help?" Karl asked through a yawn.

Gretchen shook her head, concentrating on milking.

"Not at all?"

"Tante Klegg usually helps, but she's helping Mama this morning." Gretchen's voice held a heavy warning not to question further. "Are you sure you don't know how to milk a cow?"

"How can you even see what you're doing?" Karl said, waving at the low, flickering light of the kerosene lamp. "Why not wait until daybreak?"

"And make this poor girl suffer more?" Gretchen demanded. "We always milk her before daybreak, rain or shine, searing heat or freezing wind. It would be cruel to make her wait."

Karl stared at the cow's big lashes. "Never thought about a cow suffering."

Gretchen leaned back on her squat stool and peered around the cow's front to stare at Karl. "You weren't raised on a farm then."

Karl shrugged. "Not a farm with cows at least."

With a thoughtful nod, Gretchen disappeared behind the cow. "We used to grow grain, but with Papa and Werner gone, it was too much to keep track of. We rent out the fields until they return. What do you know about growing grain?"

"Nothing," Karl admitted. He sat in the straw, leaning his back against the barn wall.

Sunlight began to peek through a crack in the mortar holding the wall together. Karl watched, fascinated by the way the light danced across the dirt floor.

A piece of straw turned to gold and back again. A dirt clod grew interesting shadows, almost making a face, and then was nothing but a pile of dirt again. Gretchen's hair was brilliant fire, braided high atop her head, and then calmed to a dull red.

There was something so interesting about light. Karl could not put his finger on why he was so obsessed. Colors, too. He loved identifying the names of different colors, even without telling anyone. Gretchen's dress, for instance, was a rich chocolate. It contrasted with the dirt in the barn, which was more of a dusty, discarded gray.

Karl did not want to admit to anyone he kept naming colors. He was too afraid they might think him mad. What sort of a person catalogued colors instead of fighting to regain his memories?

"Do you know how to grow anything?" Gretchen asked, starting to sound irritated. "If I asked you to weed a garden, would you?"

"Send someone else to do it, you mean?"

The milking noises stopped. Karl chuckled.

"Well, at least I've learned you think you're funny," Gretchen said. She lifted the bucket, only half full, and motioned at him to follow her. "I have to take this to the ice box, then we need to feed the chickens."

Karl saluted Gretchen, limping behind her. His ankles still hurt from the ropes they bound him with, but he refused to be more of a burden to Gretchen. Anyway, if he was ever going to leave, he had to regain strength.

He was glad Tante Klegg had shoved soup and stew down his throat. He was starting to heal. He had his head wrapped still, but the bleeding had stopped. His arm and leg ached. Gretchen had applied poultices that burned, so that had to mean they were doing something.

It would not be long before Karl would be strong enough to continue south. That was, if he could escape Alina's schemes.

"Where am I, by the way?" Karl asked.

Gretchen's expression was clear: she thought he was an idiot. "On my farm," she said.

He rolled his eyes. "You know that's not what I mean. Thanks to Alina, I know I'm in Ohio. I didn't even know that at Camp Chase. We were all too tired to care where we were when we got there."

Gretchen handed him the pail, which was lighter than it looked, and waved at him to keep walking. She avoided looking at him. "We're close to Grove City; it's a small town. It's where we buy goods and go to church."

Karl's blank stare did not surprise Gretchen. He was a Confederate; he did not know or care about Ohio towns.

"You must have walked about five miles to get here. That's about how far Grove City is from Camp Chase as the crow flies. Do you remember Columbus? That's where you would have taken a train from Camp Chase."

Karl shifted the pail from one hand to the other. "That makes sense. Everyone said the prison was four miles from the city. They must've been talking about Columbus. But I've never been there. Don't think I made it a mile out of the prison before they gave up on me."

Gretchen opened the kitchen door. "Well, you walked far enough to collapse in my garden. I guess that was pretty far in your condition."

She set up a bowl on the table and spread cheesecloth on top of it. She took the milk pail from Karl and poured the bucket over the bowl to strain it of the fat, foam, and other surface dirt. Karl watched, fascinated. She motioned for him to open the ice box, which was little more than a metal box submerged in the ground to keep milk cool. He retrieved the empty glass bottle. Gretchen filled it with the cleaned milk and capped it. She rinsed the bucket out with water.

"You were in the war," she said finally. "Wouldn't you have walked from battle to battle?"

Karl followed as she trotted back to the barn. He said nothing as she grabbed a burlap bag and tossed the corn and watched the chickens scramble around for their share.

"Do you think everyone's serious about us marrying?" Karl asked instead of answering, since he did not know the answer.

"My aunt will do anything to keep the family from ruin. She cares a lot about reputation. Mama'd be glad to be rid of me, even to a Confederate." Gretchen laughed. "My papa's the only one who saw me as worth anything. Even Werner thought I was his pesky sister who never could avoid trouble."

She hung the burlap bag on its nail. "It's not like I look for trouble. I just... I don't know. I have to learn things the hard way, I guess."

Karl nodded. "I live in that world."

Gretchen glanced at him over her shoulder, her expression suspicious.

He held up his hands. "I mean it. If I could learn who I was, I would, wouldn't I? Instead, I have to wait around. I have to make mistakes and put other people in danger. You think I enjoy this?"

"Well, you're a Confederate, aren't you? Isn't it a pleasure to know you could sentence three Unionist women to death for housing you?" Though the words were accusatory, Gretchen's tone was genuinely curious.

Karl sighed. "There were many reasons to be a Confederate. I knew southerners who were Unionist in the prison. I suppose you know Yankees who are sympathetic to their Confederate kin?"

Gretchen shifted her weight and would not look at him, confirming his suspicion.

"If there's one thing I remember from the war and about prison, it's that nothing's as clear as we want to believe. It's muddy. I heard Yankee boys complaining about how they went to war to save the Union, not to free the slaves."

Gretchen nodded. "That was why Werner left. All his friends went off to war when spirits were high. They were going to protect the Union, keep the states together."

"I don't know why I went to war," Karl admitted. "But I don't have many thoughts about slaves or slavery, so I don't know that I went off to protect the Confederacy."

Gretchen looked at him askance. "How do I know you're not saying that to protect your own hide?"

Karl shrugged. "I guess you don't. What about your pa? Why did he leave?"

Gretchen stiffened. "He went to war for moral reasons."

"Keeping the union together isn't moral?"

"Not if the union is corrupt. Which isn't what Pa said was happening, but he did say the country was poisoned."

Karl rubbed his chin. There had been a book thumper in the prison that used to talk about slavery like it was poisoning the country. Something about a proclamation that was the first step to a true cleanse. "So your pa was abolitionist. What did he think of the... proclamation, then?"

Gretchen stared at him, eyes wide. "What do you know about abolitionism and proclamations?"

"Camp Chase." He shrugged. "There were more than Confederates in that prison. There were defectors and deserters and all sorts of men there." He scratched the bandage holding his head together. "Your brother might even be one of them, if he got all mad about the war changing under his feet. Have you asked?"

"Have I—? Ooh, you shut your mouth," Gretchen breathed, picking up her bucket and stomping to the other end of the garden. "My brother would never desert the army because of the proclamation. It didn't even free the slaves in the Union, only the Confederate states. Who could get upset about that?"

"What did I say?" Karl asked, tottering after her with his limp. "Didn't mean to upset you. Wouldn't be alive without your help."

"And Mama would love to count that in her list of reasons why I marry you and get out of her hair," Gretchen said. "How can you remember stupid things like the proclamation, and abolitionists? What about your name?" She grabbed her skirts and scrambled to standing. "Who cares about why Werner and Papa went to war anyway? They're gone, and they might never come back. But you," she pointed her finger at him, "you're here. And you might have killed the president. And I struck my pastor's daughter, Karl! And—oh Lord, my pastor thinks I'm going to marry you!"

Karl blinked, unsure what to do. He did not much care what the pastor or anyone else thought Gretchen was going to do. But he did want to know, more than he cared to admit, whether Gretchen thought he was worth marrying.

FIFTEEN

Monday, 17 April 1865 / Grove City, Ohio

Gretchen skidded to a halt on the porch when she heard her mother and aunt arguing again. Arguing was all anyone did anymore. She had thought, with the war ending, that the arguments would stop.

"Alina tells us that our Werner returns, and yet we are still harboring that… that criminal," her mother said.

"Either you believe Alina that Werner is coming home," Tante Klegg said, "or you do not believe her, and I never want to hear her name again. I cannot listen to your hysterics about that girl's betrayal much longer."

"You can listen a little longer. It has only been one day."

Tante Klegg snorted.

"Whether Werner returns to us or not," Gretchen's mother insisted, "we still have the problem of the criminal."

"We do not know he is the criminal," Tante Klegg said. She, like her sister, refused to name the man who murdered Mr. Lincoln.

"It hurts my heart," Gretchen's mother said. "My son and husband went to war for Mr. Lincoln. Yet his killer pulls weeds with our daughter."

Gretchen inched closer to the window so she could peek into the kitchen.

Tante Klegg rubbed her temples. "This is not our first war, or have you so soon forgotten?"

An uncomfortable silence fell.

Karl caught up with Gretchen on the porch. He bent, his hands on his knees and his shoulders heaving as he panted. Gretchen threw her hand over his mouth. She shook her head, hoping her mother and aunt did not know they were eavesdropping.

Karl stopped breathing.

Gretchen dropped her hand as if his lips burned her. Karl shoved his hands in his pockets. He would not look at Gretchen, which was fine by her because it was exasperating to feel embarrassed by a boy.

"I know, I know, how could I forget? Our parents dying of cholera. Our poor brother Baldemar, conscripted to the army. Without your clever thinking, I never would have met Gregory. We would not be in America at all," her mother said.

Gretchen wiped her hands on her apron. She knew her mother and aunt had left Germany under sad circumstances, but that was it. She never would have guessed her grandparents had died of cholera. She had no idea she once had an uncle.

What else had they kept from her?

"Yes," Tante Klegg said. "I have always taken care of you. Do you think I would risk all that we have for one of Gretchen's schemes? I will figure something out with Karl."

"Well, if you know so much, what are we to do about the warden?" her mother asked.

Karl dropped his hands from his pockets and pressed his ear to the wall. Gretchen exchanged a worried glance with him. Apparently, they had spent too much time in the barn and missed a warden's surprise visit. What luck.

Tante Klegg was silent.

"He knows," her mother said, insistent. "This warden, he comes to our farm because he knows we have this Karl." She spat his name out like spoiled milk.

"I do not think he was a warden at all," Tante Klegg said. "He was a boy shaking in his boots. He did not want his captain to discover he lost prisoners during the exchange."

Gretchen held her breath. Maybe Karl was telling the truth after all that he was not Mr. Lincoln's infamous killer. That should please her mother.

"Who would honor those exchanges now that Mr. Lincoln is dead?" her mother said. "Why would we send one more murderer home to hunt after my husband and son?"

"Because the exchange for Karl could have been for your husband or son," Tante Klegg said.

Gretchen's mother gasped, though she could not tell whether it was from shock, dismay, or disgust.

"That boy searches the countryside because he lost three prisoners," Tante Klegg said. "It was an even exchange, a Unionist for a Confederate, and the Confederates want what they think is due to them."

Muffled sniffles came from Gretchen's mother.

"They do not know we have Karl," Tante Klegg said.

Gretchen peeked through a gap in the doorway hinge. Tante Klegg had her back to the door, but it was clear she held her crying sister in her arms.

"Selfish, these men," Gretchen's mother whined into her aunt's shoulder. "Running around shooting at each other to prove a point. I cannot understand them."

"We are not meant to, else we would be men ourselves," Tante Klegg said.

"Do you believe if we returned Karl to Camp Chase, Gregory or Werner would come home?" Gretchen's mother asked.

Gretchen shivered, seeing them for the first time. They were not her aunt and mother only, she realized. They were sisters. They were immigrants in a strange land holding onto all that remained of their family.

"I do not think it is possible to know," Tante Klegg said.

Gretchen's mind raced. She had not thought Karl could be a deterrent to her brother's and father's return. Last she knew, they were not prisoners of war.

They could return before Karl left, though. Gretchen shivered. For all she knew, Werner and her father might start the war again at the sight of a Confederate in their house.

If there was one thing Karl had taught Gretchen, it was that nothing matched expectation. She could not expect her father to be the gentle philosopher or her brother the family favorite.

Gretchen looked up to find Karl watching her, wary. She motioned for him to follow her as she tiptoed back to the barn.

Once out of earshot, Gretchen grabbed Karl's arm. "I don't think you're John Wilkes Booth!"

He looked down at her hand on his arm. "Who?"

Gretchen frowned, not understanding why he was not as excited as she. She dropped her hand as realization struck.

Of course, Karl would not know the name of John Wilkes Booth. He did not have access to their newspaper; her mother ensured that. And no one ever mentioned the murderer's name out of superstitious spite. One did not invoke the devil's name.

"John Wilkes Booth," Gretchen explained. "The man who killed the president."

Karl nodded. "Guess it is a good thing to know who I'm not, on the way to knowing who I am."

Gretchen shrugged, the excitement wearing off. Karl made a good point. She only knew who he was not. She did not know if he was a killer, philosopher, farmer, businessman. He was a nameless, hopeless, Confederate.

"He's the one who killed the president?" Karl asked. "Your president?"

"Yours too," Gretchen reminded him. She punched his arm and he stumbled. "The Confederates surrendered last week."

Karl cleared his throat, rubbing where she hit him. "Guess I should work on not saying things like that."

"You can't say things like that around Alina or Pastor Baumbach. Or anyone. You can't make mistakes like that. You're a part of the Union now."

Karl traced the edge of the bandage still wrapped near his temple. Something about what she said rang in his mind. When he left the prison, he could not leave until pledging his allegiance.

"Part of the Union," Karl echoed. He shook his head. He lost the memory, whatever it was. He kicked a tuft of grass and shoved his hands in his pant pockets. "You said your pastor thinks you're marrying me."

Gretchen planted her hands on her hips. "And?"

He did not like her accusatory tone. "I'm asking what you want. If you want to marry me."

Gretchen's expression was wary.

"Well, I mean, if you want to pretend you're marrying me. So I can get strong enough to leave."

Gretchen took one of her braids and fussed with the string keeping it together. "I can't lie to my pastor."

"Your family seemed fine lying to him, and in the church no less. And you've lied plenty since I've known you. What's so different?"

"I don't lie to my pastor," Gretchen insisted. "And I don't think my aunt and mother lied to him, either. As long as you're around, they're going to marry me to you."

He saw the determined glint in her eye. Gretchen was going to help him; that was for sure. Either she would help him remember, or help him leave. Anything to avoid to marrying him. Karl knew he should have felt glad—relieved even. So it was more than a mite uncomfortable that what Karl felt was stung.

OUR NATIONAL AFFLICTION

Tuesday, 18 April 1865 / The Ohio Daily Statesman

Owing to the suspension of business after the announcement of Mr. Lincoln's death, we have no Cincinnati or Cleveland Market Reports this morning.

OUR NATIONAL AFFLICTION. We have been accustomed from infancy to read of the murder and assassination of kings, princes, and rulers in former times and in other lands. But we never dreamed that such foul crimes would come home to us, and be perpetrated by Americans on American soil. Yet the hand of the assassin has struck down the President of the Republic, and nearly taken the life of our Chief Minister of State, and that of one of his assistants.

This is the saddest, most deplorable and awful event that has occurred in our whole history, from the birth of the nation in July, 1776, to the present moment. It may lead to consequences the most frightful, upon which we dare not reflect, much less write.

Nothing but the overruling hand of that Providence upon which our Fathers relied in the darkest hour of trial can avert those consequences, and save our people from becoming the prey of anarchy, ultimating in an iron despotism.

SIXTEEN

Tuesday, 18 April 1865 / Grove City, Ohio

It was Tuesday when Gretchen got a copy of Monday's newspaper. She had sneaked to the neighbors instead of doing chores to bribe the youngest child for their copy. Gretchen chafed to know more about the president. She was days behind what it felt like the entire world knew. She had to know how John Wilkes Booth assaulted Mr. Lincoln. She wanted to know how Booth escaped and how terrible the president's last minutes were.

Gretchen hid in the hayloft with the *Ohio Daily Statesman.* Her hands shook as she spread the newspaper open.

"Assassination of President Lincoln and Secretary Seward—Full Particulars," the headline screamed.

Thick black ink filled the newspaper margins. It was the newspaper's way of showing mourning. It was like the entire paper wore a sheath of black, and it was difficult to read the paragraphs between.

Gretchen squinted, angling the paper so she could read it in the slivered sunlight. She tried to imagine the world's chaos outside her little farm.

The *Statesman* described how Booth was identified by his discarded hat and boot spur. Karl had no boots, and his head injury prevented a hat.

Somehow, Booth escaped despite panicked onlookers patrolling and picketing the streets. The *Statesman* described the attack on the Secretary of State, Mr. Seward, in his home. Everyone presumed the poor man had died along with Mr. Lincoln. Andy Johnson's manner was solemn and dignified when sworn in as president. The entire matter was a national calamity. Booth and his compatriot, John Surratt, had apparently intended to flee to Canada.

And then there were the special dispatches from sister newspapers...

The *Cincinnati Gazette* claimed Surratt stabbed Secretary Seward and his son, Major Seward.

Their second dispatch described the Lincolns attending the play *Our American Cousin*. The bullet came out of Mr. Lincoln's temple, and Mrs. Lincoln fainted at the sight. The assailant was a man. He was about thirty years (too old for Karl) and five feet tall (too short for Karl). He had a spare build (that could have been Karl), with fair skin and a large, dark moustache.

Gretchen was certain Karl could not grow much more than the stubble gracing his gaunt face. They had yet to find a shaving blade for him because he had not needed it.

By one in the morning on Friday, the poor president was senseless with little hope of recovery. That was the same night Gretchen had collapsed in bed after celebrating the war's end with dancing and bonfires. By the time Gretchen had fallen asleep, the president's physicians knew he was dying.

New York described a city of "intense sorrow...depicted on all countenances." All flags were at half-mast by nine in the morning. Everyone directed their utmost rage at all known secessionists and rebel sympathizers. Voters decided thirteen "lucky" citizens would represent the city at the president's funeral.

Gretchen wiped tears from her face with the back of her hand, still dirty from weeding. She knew this was what her aunt and mother were afraid of. This was not the time to have associations with rebel sympathizers. No one wanted to be at the mercy of vengeful crowds, including Gretchen.

Gretchen did not want to be another Mary Surratt, or given her nickname, "mistress of the devil's work." Gretchen was a loyal patriot, and she wanted to do right by her countrymen. She knew the nation needed to heal. What she did not know was how that could be possible without Abraham Lincoln to guide everyone.

Cities around the nation mourned the president's death as the news reached them. Indianapolis reported all forms of business had stopped. Owners closed doors and covered windows with black crepe minutes after the announcement.

Nashville's parade celebrating the surrender had just begun when the news hit the city. The parade broke down. Soldiers returned to camp with their firearms reversed, marching instead to a dirge.

Baltimore crowds had grown rowdy and indignant. Someone found "obnoxious pictures" of John Wilkes Booth and smashed bricks through a photographer's shop window. Gretchen shook her head. The day before, those photos must have brought customers. Who had not wanted a photo of the famous Baltimore actor, John Wilkes Booth?

What a difference a day—a choice—made to so many people.

Gretchen shivered, even though a moment before her palms had been sweaty. She stared at the paper in her hand until the letters blurred. The scattered news reports made it clear that this was not the result of one decision.

John Wilkes Booth had put a lot of thought into taking the president's life. He had thought about it so much, he had George Atzerodt attempt to kill the vice president and Lewis Powell attempt to kill the secretary of state. What a stroke of luck that Atzerodt turned out to be terrible at stabbing vital organs and that Powell chickened out entirely.

The fact was, Booth tried to destroy the Union in one fell swoop. Booth wanted the war to continue after the Confederate surrender.

Gretchen dropped the newspaper and brought her palms together. "Lord," she whispered, "I know I don't ask for your counsel much. I let Tante Klegg and Mama do that for me. But these stories... they tell me the world doesn't know which way is up anymore."

"Please don't make the war go another four years."

Her voice broke, but she kept her palms pressed together. "And please help Karl know who he is. It doesn't feel right sending him away if he doesn't know who he is or where he's going. But the longer he's here, the more danger we're in. So please, watch over us, too, and keep us in your grace."

There was no gesture or signal that anyone had heard, but that was all right. Gretchen figured if her little prayer did any good at all, it was worth the time.

She picked up the newspaper, dusting it with her apron hem. The advertisement in the bottom corner caught her eye. It was the only positive news in the entire sheet. Dry goods prices were dropping for the first time since the war began. They would have to think about replenishing their sugar stores.

That sent Gretchen scouring the newspaper for other tidbits of good news. Anything to combat the overwhelming hopelessness that caused her shoulders to droop.

And there it was, halfway down page four. Secretary Seward and Major Seward had survived their attacks. And Vice President—well, President—Johnson had evaded an attack altogether. It all appeared linked to Booth's original assassination plan.

Gretchen leaned back, her eyes closed. She listened to the chickens below her clucking amongst themselves. Those dumb birds. Gretchen wondered how much her aunt and mother knew, and how much they had chosen not to tell her.

The sudden creaking sound of the barn door opening made Gretchen freeze. She crawled across the hayloft on all fours, intending to snatch the ladder.

By the time Gretchen untangled her skirts and spit the straw from her mouth, Karl was halfway up the ladder. It was short, five rungs, so even a man of his little strength could make the climb.

"Well," Karl said, plopping onto a bale beside her, "your ma and aunt gave me an earful. They know we heard them yesterday."

"And how would they know that?" Gretchen said, her tone accusatory. She yanked her skirt away from his muddy foot. For some reason, he preferred to go barefoot. Not that she minded; she preferred to be barefoot herself. But if her aunt saw her dirty skirts, it would be her turn for an earful.

"Because they couldn't hear us arguing," Karl replied as if it were the most sensible thing in the world. "The farm was so quiet, they figured we was eavesdropping."

She stared at him.

"I mean, we *was* eavesdropping."

"I know," Gretchen retorted. She tucked the newspaper under her skirt. Better that she be the only one aware of things for now. "I got to hear all about an uncle I didn't know existed." She did not like the soft expression she saw move across his face and linger. "What?"

"You've been crying."

"Not about that." Her expression turned rueful. "Why would I cry about a man I never met? I didn't have an uncle yesterday. I guess I still don't have one today."

Karl shrugged. "Why would you befriend a Confederate and bring him in your home? I don't pretend to know you, but you got to admit you have a pattern of pretending you don't care when you do. A lot."

Gretchen grabbed a fistful of straw and threw it at him. "Who cares about your patterns?" She meant to sound more cross than she did. In truth, she was a little pleased Karl had noticed such a thing about her, if only because no one else seemed to.

Karl wiped the straw off his lap and smiled.

"What's our punishment for eavesdropping, then?" Gretchen asked. "Confess to the pastor and ask for absolution?"

"Do what now?"

Gretchen waved her hand at him. "It's Tante Klegg's favorite thing about being Lutheran, confessing her sins. She makes me do it all the time, but no one else confesses these days. That's for grandparents. Go on, what's our punishment?"

He shook his head. He picked apart a piece of straw and would not look at her.

Come on," Gretchen teased, "it can't be worse than a counterfeit engagement."

"You got to teach me how to run the farm in case your father and brother don't come back," he said in a rush.

Gretchen was dumbstruck. "But we know Werner is coming back. Alina said as much."

"They said it would build up my strength. And your character."

"My character's plenty strong," Gretchen said.

"Well, I suppose there's strong character, and then there's strong-willed," Karl recited.

"Tante Klegg told you to say that," Gretchen said.

"Yes, ma'am, she did."

Gretchen sighed. "Well, come on then. It's time to find the eggs anyway."

Karl frowned. "You mean, the chickens?" He curled his fingers into his palms.

"What's wrong?" Gretchen said, crawling to the ladder. "You got something against chickens?"

"I don't, but they got something against me," he said.

UNREPENTANT LEADERS TO BE PUNISHED

Tuesday, 18 April 1865 / The Ohio Daily Statesman

PRESIDENT JOHNSON TO BE MERCIFUL TO THE PEOPLE OF THE REBEL STATES—UNREPENTANT LEADERS TO BE PUNISHED.

The Post's special says President Johnson yesterday said to a clergyman who begged of him to be merciful to the rebels, that mercy to individuals was not always mercy to the State. He also declared to a prominent member of Congress that he was willing to act with the utmost magnanimity towards the common people of the rebel States, but that the unrepentant leaders must be punished.

DEVELOPMENTS OF ONE OF THE CONSPIRATORS

Tuesday, 18 April 1865 / The Ohio Daily Statesman

It is understood that the party alluded to as under arrest here, states that the original design of the conspirators was merely to capture President Lincoln, some time back, and make him a prisoner, and in this way compel a general release of all rebel prisoners then held by the United States.

When the general exchange of prisoners commenced, this project was abandoned by him and others as no longer necessary, and he says he refused to have anything further to do with it and endeavored to induce others to give up their designs upon the life of the President...

A FALSE AND DASTARDLY CHARGE

Wednesday, 19 April 1865 / The Ohio Daily Statesman

*The Journal of Tuesday morning, in an article headed "The Rule of Suc-
cession," says, referring to the assassination of President Lincoln and the
attempt to assassinate Secretary Seward:*

*"Those not actually engaged in the rebellion, but who, from partisan
ties or other considerations, have been inclined to apologize for those
engaged in it, and palliate their offense, should now feel themselves called
upon to come out from those associations and renounce all fealty to a
party having such proclivities.*

*For although Democrats, as a party, may disclaim the act, and but
few of the party are probably directly responsible for the enormity in
which it has culminated, yet it is a fact that the assassination is distinctly
traceable to the teachings of that party, and it behooves all honest men
who are disinclined to share in such grave responsibility, to separate from
the association of those who are to a greater or less degree answerable for
the act aimed, as well at the life of the nation, as that of the President."*

*Here are two distinct and explicit charges brought against the Democ-
ratic party as a class of citizens, and against every man belonging to it:*

1. *That Democrats are inclined to apologize for those engaged in rebellion, and palliate their offense.*
2. *That the assassination of the President is DISTINCTLY traceable to the teachings of the Democratic party.*

As to both these charges, and other malicious insinuations contained in the foregoing extract from The Journal, we brand them as false and infamous, and charge that the editor of The Journal knew them to be such when he wrote them down.

SEVENTEEN

Tuesday, 18 - Wednesday, 25 April 1865 / Grove City, Ohio

While the world lost its mind hunting for John Wilkes Booth, Gretchen studied Karl. At first, she had thought he could help her. There were many chores and only her hands, since her aunt tended the farmhouse and her mother refused to leave her bedroom.

One thing was clear: Karl was not a dairy or chicken farmer, that was certain. Or if he were, he was terrible at it. It was not just that he pulled plants thinking they were weeds. He did not know how to milk a cow or pull eggs from a chicken without losing an eye.

Gretchen supposed Karl might have been a crop or horse or sheep farmer, except he got spooked any time an animal his size or larger came too close. Karl's lack of skill drove Gretchen to distraction.

And he daydreamed. All. The. Time. Gretchen told Karl to get water from the well only to find him half an hour later staring at a cobweb. When asked what he was doing, Karl said something about water droplets caught on the strands. When sent to pick kindling for the stove, he disappeared for an hour. Gretchen found him studying the veins of a leaf in the sunlight. She could not understand his obsession with light.

Karl's hands were not meant for farming, or not yet anyway. His hands lacked calluses; he had town hands, like a shopkeeper.

It went like this for a week. Gretchen would hand something to Karl to test him. He would panic and refuse to try, or surprise her with his skill, or wander off to sit and think alone.

Last week, it had seemed so easy to bring Karl into the house. He needed help, and she looked to help. Her aunt, for whatever reason, had gone along with it, only to turn on her as soon as Karl was trouble.

The newspaper clipping describing John Wilkes Booth stayed in Gretchen's pocket. She could not figure out why she hesitated to tell her aunt and mother about it. They rarely read the newspaper. The only reading material in the house was their Lutheran Bible, and that was in German. Gretchen felt confident her family did not know how unlike Karl was to John Wilkes Booth. Yet rather than rushing to tell them, she kept it to herself.

Deep down, Gretchen knew it was because she had only confirmed they did not know anything about Karl. He had been at Camp Chase. He might have been a prisoner left by the wayside. The authorities might throw them all into prison for not turning him in right away.

Gretchen stared at the ceiling of her bed that night. Knowing Karl was not John Wilkes Booth did not seem to solve anyway. Karl had been a Confederate, which was as almost as bad as shooting the president anyway.

Gretchen counted the cobwebs in the rafters above her bed. Karl had pointed them out to her earlier in the day. He showed her they were not annoying wisps that caught her hair, they had patterns. They sparkled in the light and danced in the night breeze.

Well, they would have, if there were a breeze. The night air was stuffy despite the window being open. There was no cross breeze, and Gretchen sweltered in her nightshift. Her thoughts tossed and turned because her body was too hot and sweaty. Every move she made caused her thin, wet mattress to squeak against the ropes. It was a hot, terrible night, and she suffered from hot, terrible thoughts.

Without the drama of harboring a criminal, babysitting Karl was tedious. Gretchen had to change his bandages and teach him to help with chores. She had to endure him following her around because he was afraid of staying in the house with her family.

Well, that was not true or fair anymore. It had been tedious at first. Gretchen now understood her brother's annoyance when she chatted his ear off around the farm.

Karl did not chat her ear off, though, she spent all of her time talking to him. Gretchen found she liked to say ridiculous things if it meant Karl might smirk. That was as far as he went, smiling-wise. And it *had* been annoying earlier in the week, but now Gretchen liked when Karl made her stop and look at something. He sure knew how to paint words.

As she struggled to catch sleep, Gretchen wondered what Karl was thinking about. He had earned the privilege of not sleeping every night tied to the chair. Instead, he crawled into the hayloft with a thin blanket to protect him from scratches. It puzzled her, wondering what a man without memories did to fall asleep.

Did he recite children's rhymes until his lids were heavy? Did he plot his escape, assuming he still considered them his captors rather than his friends?

Gretchen sat upright and knocked her head into the roof beam above her. It was one thing to wonder whether Karl considered them captors or friends. When had she changed her mind from being his captor to being his friend?

Karl was dangerous, but not because he shot the president. Gretchen resolved to tell her aunt and mother in the morning that Karl was not John Wilkes Booth. She knew it would mean they would kick Karl out of the house. They would have to.

And then Gretchen could stop her little flights of fancy. They did not happen all the time. Now that she had built up Karl's confidence to do little chores that did not wear him out, she found herself watching him. The trouble with watching was it led to daydreaming.

Sometimes, Gretchen imagined Karl taking her hand and walking along the creek's edge. No aunt, no mother, no assassination, and no war. Just the two of them, talking about things they read, and places they wanted to see.

Gretchen rubbed her forehead and stifled a groan. She was starting to sound like Alina.

Patriots did not go around developing feelings for their prisoners. It was nonsense. And Gretchen, while she would admit she was spontaneous, she was not nonsensical.

EIGHTEEN

Tuesday, 25 April 1865 / Grove City, Ohio

It was now nine days since the president had died. Gretchen decided it was time her aunt and mother knew Karl was not the murderer. It was time for Karl to leave, before she started making a fool of herself.

Gretchen pulled the newspaper clipping from her pocket as she entered the kitchen. The edges were well-worn, and the black-filled margins had faded to gray.

Tante Klegg and her mother sat at the table, resting their foreheads in their palms.

"Mama?" Gretchen said. She brushed her fingers on her mother's shoulder and placed the clipping on the table.

Her mother took it, her expression impassive in the waning sunlight.

"He didn't kill the president," Gretchen whispered. She did not know why she was whispering. Karl slept in the barn.

Her aunt stared at her. "Of course, he did not."

Gretchen froze. Her thoughts skidded to a halt. She tried to understand why Tante Klegg looked at her like she was a fool. All Gretchen could think was how much she hated Tante Klegg sometimes. Always so righteous, so sensible, so ready to correct Gretchen.

"Did you believe a man in his condition could travel from Washington to Grove City overnight?" Tante Klegg asked.

Her mother tore the newspaper. "We have known all along," she said. Her tone was so nonchalant it made Gretchen want to scream.

Instead, Gretchen said, "You *swore* that he killed the president!"

"He did!" her mother said. She lifted her skirts so Gretchen could see her grind her heel into the shredded paper. "They all did. Every last one who stood against this nation. Every last one who shot a bullet at my husband and son. They tried to ruin this country, and they killed the president in their plot to do so."

"I will say that whatever this Karl was, he could not have been a soldier. He cowers from a gun," Tante Klegg said. She turned to stoke the fire for dinner.

This was not going the way Gretchen had imagined it. After her revelation, she expected her mother and aunt to show shock or surprise or relief. She expected them to say how long Karl could remain on the farm. She expected them to make plans so they could all move on with their lives.

"What do you know about soldiers, anyway?" Gretchen burst.

"I know enough," Tante Klegg said, her tone forbidding Gretchen to press further.

"Does it have to do with how my uncle died?" Gretchen regretted saying anything as soon as it left her mouth.

Tante Klegg lost color, and her mother grabbed the table to stay upright.

"What do you know of Baldemar?" her aunt asked.

"You have no right to mention him," her mother said.

"Why not?" Gretchen said. "Why wouldn't you tell me I have—had—an uncle?"

"Because of who killed him." Tante Klegg's soft tone silenced Gretchen.

"It was Edelgard's *verlobter*," her mother said. "He went against his friends and family, and our Baldemar suffered for it. Died for it. You want to know what it is to have a friend kill your brother? You want to know what it is for the *verlobter* of your sister to kill your brother? You will know if Werner returns and that—that *Karl* remains here."

This was more than Gretchen anticipated. Not only did she have a long dead uncle, but her aunt had not always been a spinster. Someone in this world, once upon a time, had wanted to marry Tante Klegg. And that same someone was why Gretchen no longer had an uncle.

Gretchen stepped back. She bumped into Karl, who stood in the doorway. She did not have to ask whether he had heard. "Karl wouldn't kill anyone," Gretchen said. She turned to Tante Klegg. "You said yourself he isn't a soldier."

"But Werner is," Tante Klegg pointed out.

"Werner wouldn't kill Karl, either," Gretchen said.

"War does things to people," Karl said behind her. "Can't know how Werner will be once he's come home."

"He speaks the truth," Tante Klegg said. Her voice hardened. "The same way Karl does not know who he is, Werner may have forgotten. Or, Werner saw so many things that he does not want to remember."

Gretchen stared at the tears in Tante Klegg's eyes. Tante Klegg never cried.

Tante Klegg could burn herself on the stove. She could stick herself with a knife. She could trip and land on her face. It did not matter; she would get right back to whatever she was doing as if nothing had happened.

"Is that why you came to the United States?" Gretchen asked. She ignored Tante Klegg's downcast eyes and her prayers for forgiveness.

"We came here because we had nowhere else to go," her mother said. "Our parents died before any of this happened. I thank the Lord for that. But when Edelgard's *verlobter* did what he did, we could not stay with family. She chose her partner like you choose yours, with patriotic fervor."

"I don't know what you're talking about," Gretchen said."I haven't chosen anyone."

"Well," Karl said, "you did choose to bring me into your home."

"Will you shut up?" Gretchen said.

"It is a decision I regret," Tante Klegg retorted, glaring at her sister, "but only because of its terrible ending." She turned to Gretchen, her expression beseeching. "This is why you must marry Karl."

Gretchen's mouth went dry. "What does this have to do with me and Karl?"

"What else?" her mother said, annoyance and sarcasm spearing each word. "My sister cannot make a mistake. And if she does... heaven help us all, she will keep trying until she gets it right. You are her chance to fix her mistakes. You, my little Gretchen, are her salvation."

Tante Klegg lifted the kettle so she could slam it down onto the stove. "Do not speak blasphemy, Adelaide!"

Karl cleared his throat. "Not to be a nuisance, ma'am, but... I'm not understanding this at all. How does me marrying or not marrying Gretchen help Ms. Klegg?"

Gretchen's mother blinked as if seeing Karl for the first time. "My brother and her *verlobter*—they died before their time because of her."

"The war?" Gretchen breathed. She had heard time and again how the threat of war in the Germanic states had chased them to America back in the 1840s.

Her mother's laugh was cruel and mirthless. "No! Baldemar caught Edelgard in a… in a… a *compromising* position! My older sister who could do no wrong!" She pointed a shaking finger at Tante Klegg. Every word was more strident. "My brother challenged her *verlobter* to a duel. Stupid, proud boy, he should have left Edelgard to her fate. Her *verlobter* accepted the duel. He killed my brother and then himself."

"What?" Karl exclaimed. "Why would he do that?"

"My Alric, he killed my brother," Tante Klegg explained. She ran her hands down her apron front, smoothing wrinkles that were not there. "Alric knew I could never marry him."

Gretchen's head swiveled back to her mother. This was worse than those novels Alina always read, except… this was not a story. This was her life. Her life built on a crumbling pile of lies and betrayals.

Her mother sniffed. "We are lucky I married the traveling American and he paid for our passage before—" A look from Tante Klegg silenced her.

Gretchen's head spun. She had thought Tante Klegg had found passage out of a war-ridden Germanic state by her cunning. She had thought her mother married her father long after their arrival in Ohio.

"You'd marry your niece to a man without a past and an unknown future so you could say… what?" Karl said, when neither Gretchen's mother nor Tante Klegg continued.

"Better married than living off the charity of bitter, resentful family," Tante Klegg said. She threw her arms wide. "Gretchen is too like me. She will end up alone and dependent because she is so stubborn."

"I am nothing like you," Gretchen said.

"Oh, but you are," Tante Klegg said. With a long, slow exhale, she admitted, "Because you are my daughter."

NINETEEN

Tuesday, 25 April 1865 / Grove City, Ohio

Gretchen had always thought those girls who fainted in Alina's books were plain silly. It felt odd to want to faint and be jealous of those girls who knew the exact moment when to faint and make it count. Fainting had to be better than what she was doing, which amounted to a whole lot of nothing.

"Did you hear me?" Tante Klegg said.

Gretchen blinked. She could not think of an answer because she had so many questions of her own. Of course, she had heard Tante Klegg. But she had not understood.

"What do you mean?" Karl said. He put his hand on Gretchen's shoulder.

Gretchen did not move. She could not. She had forgotten how.

"I mean that Gretchen is my daughter," Tante Klegg said.

A sharp pain jabbed behind Gretchen's temple, and she squeezed her eyes shut. Her mind raced, trying to remember how they got to this point. She did not realize asking about an unknown uncle would destroy her family.

"We discovered my condition when we arrived in this country." Tante Klegg spoke to Karl since Gretchen would not look at her. "We could not be outcasts in our new—" She paused, struggling to master a myriad of emotions. "A foreign mother, unwed, is only meant for the poor house if she has no family to speak for her. When we settled in Grove City... Well. We never corrected assumptions. Gretchen looked like Adelaide."

Gretchen pressed her palm against her forehead. She did not understand how they could be so matter-of-fact. Tante Klegg made it sound like they were talking about weeding the garden. Gretchen felt as if her world was a pile of loose dirt at the edge of a stream, breaking in chunks to float with a mind of its own. Everything was falling apart...

Except for the things that clicked together. Gretchen did not get along with Tante Klegg. But Gretchen could read Tante Klegg's moods, because she recognized them in herself, unlike Adelaide Miller, who was a complete mystery.

No matter what Gretchen did or said, she could never win the affection of the woman who she thought was her mother. At least when Gretchen was clever, Tante Klegg would express resentful pride.

Gretchen's heart shattered. What Gretchen had interpreted as resentment was more likely sorrow. Tante Klegg could not, should not, get too close to a daughter who was not supposed to be hers. This was why her aunt and mother had warned her to not ask questions she did not want the answers to.

Her mother—well, *Tante* Miller if this was true—had never referred to Werner as Gretchen's brother. Never of her own accord, that is. That had always bothered Gretchen.

Of course, if Gretchen was Tante Klegg's daughter, then she would be Werner's cousin, not his sister. And Gretchen's father was not her father after all. He had always made a point of treating her like a beloved, trusted daughter, because he was—*is*—a good man.

Gretchen was not sure she could say the same of her aunt and mother. Were they good people for spending all these years lying to her to save their reputations in a small town?

"You married off your sister so she could be your child's respectable parent?" Karl sounded outraged.

Gretchen was grateful that Karl's thoughts mirrored her own.

Tante Klegg exchanged a glance with her sister. Gretchen felt as if they measured each other against years of wary truces.

"Adelaide's marriage to Gregory was well-timed, but not my doing," Tante Klegg said. "She was pretty and pleasant."

Gretchen glanced at Adelaide Miller, thinking how few were the times she had been pleasant over the years.

"We knew I would not get a husband unless he needed a hand at his farm. And I did not want to be someone's brood-hen or farm-hand after losing my Alric. But Adelaide," Tante Klegg continued, "she charmed the American—"

Gretchen winced, now knowing "the American" was her beloved, *adoptive* father, Gregory.

"—and he convinced himself he loved her dreams of beautiful things. Gregory was a good man, we could see that, but he was stupid to be traveling in our land during times of unrest. Of course, we saw our way out. Adelaide made Gregory promise to bring me with her." Tante Klegg glared at her sister, who glared in return. "I now know I should have remained in *Größe Deutsch* rather than suffering your foolishness all these years."

Adelaide Miller gasped. "My foolishness!"

Gretchen felt hot and cold. She both sweated and had chills running down her back. She felt stupid, and betrayed, and simple. And angry. Her head ached from all the blood pulsing through it. Gretchen was sure she was going to explode.

"All this talking and arguing and y'all never say nothing," Karl said in wonder. "You bicker and fight worse than the Rebs and Yanks and over what? A mistake from years and years ago?"

Gretchen cleared her throat. She was starting to question everything, including whether Werner was actually her older brother. "How old am I?"

"You were born in 1848," Tante Klegg replied without hesitation.

"*Mein Gott*," Gretchen swore. Tante Klegg's eyebrows shot up. "I'm the same age as Werner?"

"You are older by six months," Tante Klegg explained. "Werner was always bigger than you. It was easy to say he was your older brother."

Gretchen looked at the ceiling, determined not to let tears of frustration burst from her. This meant she was seventeen, not fifteen, and of age. No wonder Adelaide was eager to marry her off. She spun, skirts whipping around her ankles. "He knew, didn't he? Werner knew I was older than him," she shouted. "And that was why he was always so mean to me, to keep me in my place so I would never think about it."

"He could not have known," Tante Klegg protested. "We all promised each other."

A tiny noise escaped Adelaide Miller.

TWENTY

Tuesday, 25 April 1865 / Grove City, Ohio

"This is all your fault, you know," Gretchen said to Karl.

Tante Klegg had decided they did not need another body in the house to contribute to the stoked tempers. Gretchen, the ever-dutiful daughter it seemed, led Karl to the barn.

"My fault!" he exclaimed, rounding on Gretchen. He steadied himself by resting against the corner of the barn. If he moved too fast, he felt dizzy still.

"If you hadn't arrived, I never would have found out those terrible things about my family. We would have gone on as we always had." Gretchen opened the barn door and motioned for him to climb up the ladder to the hayloft.

"Because that was working for you."

Gretchen pressed her lips together, swung open the barn door, and waved him inside. As soon as he stepped out of the waning light, she followed and slammed the door behind them. "I should have reported you as soon as you fell in my garden."

Karl shook his head. "Amazing."

That was not the reaction Gretchen had expected, and she forgot what she was going to say next.

"All y'all, I don't even know *what* to call y'all, but you're confused." Karl laughed and rubbed both hands down the sides of his face. "You're more confused than I am, and I don't even know *who* I am."

"You're taking your time about knowing who you are, too," Gretchen said. "If you'd figured yourself out sooner, you'd have left by now, and I'd have the family I thought I had."

Karl pointed at her. "This ain't about me, Gretchen. Thank God it's finally not about me. And I'll remind you, I was the only one in that room standing on your side, whatever that side was."

Gretchen crossed her arms. She was not about to admit she had appreciated the way he had stood up for her, not when she was so gall-darned angry. She knew she was being unfair, but she did not know what else to do or how else to feel.

Karl placed a hand on one of the ladder rungs. "All I know is you'd have found out, one way or another, about your aunt."

"Mother," Gretchen corrected. "She claims to be my mother."

"So she does," Karl agreed. He swung his leg up and began to climb to the loft. "What do you want to do about it?"

What an odd question to ask. What *could* Gretchen do about it? Either Tante Klegg was her mother, or she was not. Either Gretchen was Tante Klegg's daughter, or she was not. There were rules about daughters and mothers in their little world.

"I need to think on it." Years of her interactions with Tante Klegg were cast in this new light. She was afraid she did not fare well. "Get up there to the hayloft. I'll let you out in the morning."

"You do that," Karl said. He climbed the last rung and dropped into the hay. "Good night, Gretchen."

Gretchen stared at the ladder, feeling alone. She knew if she did not have Karl on her side, she did not have anyone.

Her aunt and mother had shown her they only ever worried about themselves. Her father had left to fight for his ideals of what the union should be and could be, unified and without slavery. Werner thought of himself as a little hero. That had to be why he signed up for the army, despite his father's orders otherwise.

Their agendas swirled around Gretchen. They never asked what she thought or felt. Of anyone on the farm, Gretchen had to keep Karl as a friend.

She waited to hear rustling in the hay. Gretchen figured Karl had had enough for the night, and he was waiting for her to leave. She slipped out of the barn. As she fumbled with the padlock and key, a twig cracked behind her. Gretchen froze.

"You trust that boy," Tante Klegg said.

"He gave me no reason not to," Gretchen said without turning around.

"But we have? That is what you are saying," Tante Klegg said. She took the key from Gretchen and locked the barn. "Walk with me."

Sullen, Gretchen followed her to the well. She watched Tante Klegg drop the bucket into the water and crank the handle to retrieve it.

"You do not have to believe that I am your mother," Tante Klegg said. She stared into the bucket full of water, focusing on the ripples in the water from the breeze.

Gretchen could see now why Karl had thought Tante Klegg was some sort of witch. Her fierce expression was downright uncanny. Gretchen shivered in the cooling air and rubbed her arms. "I don't?"

"No, you do not. I cannot control what you think or do, the same way you cannot control me, or Alina, or my sister, or this Karl."

Gretchen crossed her arms.

"You do have to respect that I have had a large hand in your rearing. Despite my methods, you must see I made severe decisions so that you may live protected."

Gretchen made a small scoffing noise.

"This country is not kind to unwed mothers," Tante Klegg warned. "It will be better because so many young men will not return home from the war. Their wives must find ways to take care of their homes and children. When we arrived in this country, if I had told someone of my condition, I would have lost you. I could not let that happen."

Gretchen chewed her lip. This was too unlike Tante Klegg. She never explained herself. "Why are you telling me this?"

"You need to know I did these things so that I could watch over you."

"Why now?"

"Because you are of age to know. You are not a child."

Gretchen threw up her hands. "I know I'm not a child! You and Mama—" she stopped because she knew she was going to cry, and she did not want to with Tante Klegg staring at her. "I guess I need to call her Tante Miller." Gretchen pressed the heel of her hand to her forehead. "You two keep treating me like a child and all I'm trying to do is contribute. Mr. Lincoln wanted reconstruction... I guess that goes for our family, too."

Tante Klegg's eyes brightened.

"When I told you about Karl in the garden, you helped me. Why?"

"Because you said he reminded you of Werner," Tante Klegg said. She wrapped her hand around the bucket handle and hefted it from the top of the well.

"You don't even like Werner," Gretchen said. "You were always calling him a spoiled brat."

"He is a spoiled brat," Tante Klegg said. "But he is my nephew and family. You believed he was your brother, and you took his absence hard. Even though you also thought he was spoiled."

Gretchen could not deny any of that. "But as soon as we heard about Mr. Lincoln, you blamed me for bringing him into the house and got Mama all riled up. But it wasn't only me. You helped me. *We* brought Karl into the house."

Tante Klegg nodded. "And when the stakes became life threatening, you stopped consulting me. You gave him a name. You adopted him as your project. You decided you knew better. You decided he should be your friend, without knowing anything about him. All you knew was that he needed your help."

Gretchen leaned over the well, her fingers gripping the edge as she faced Tante Klegg. "What's so wrong with that?"

"I would have said nothing, if no one had gotten hurt."

"No one's going to prison. We're not conspirators, and Karl didn't shoot the president! No one got hurt!"

"Are you no one, *liebchen?*"

TWENTY-ONE

<hr>

Wednesday, 26 April 1865 / Grove City, Ohio

Harsh sunlight made Gretchen squirm under the covers. Her head pounded from nightmares about witches and conspirators and imaginary mothers. She rubbed the space between her eyes.

Sunlight. Gretchen sat up, slamming her head into the rafter above her bed. She fell back with a yelp. She had overslept. Tante Klegg was going to tan her hide. And poor Karl, trapped in the hayloft...

Gretchen scrambled around the room, throwing her petticoat and dress over her nightshift. She banged her knee on her trunk when she reached for her shoes. She did not need shoes anyway.

Gretchen tumbled down the stairs with her bodice half-buttoned. Tante Klegg was in the middle of handing Karl a plate of toasted bread.

Tante Klegg dropped the plate on the table before Karl could take it from her. "Make yourself decent!"

Gretchen whipped around so Karl could not watch as she closed the last of her buttons. She raked her fingers through her hair, throwing it into a braid so it would stop falling around her face.

Tante Klegg motioned at the chair opposite Karl. "Sit."

Too embarrassed to disobey, Gretchen slid into her seat.

"Rough night?" Karl said when Gretchen turned around again. He could have been sarcastic, but he was not. She appreciated that.

"Overslept."

Tante Klegg made a plate of toast for herself and another for Gretchen. She sat beside Karl, who shifted in his seat.

"Mama not joining us?" Gretchen said, glancing at the doorway. She noticed Tante Klegg's frown. "What? Do you want me to call her Tante Miller?"

Tante Klegg had the nerve to smile with a satisfied nod.

"What?" Gretchen said.

"I see you are more sensible than to indulge in Adelaide's dramatics." Tante Klegg crunched her toast and slurped her coffee.

Gretchen grunted. "Is the cow milked?" She blinked at the glass of milk at her place setting. There was a bowl of fresh eggs in the middle of the table. She winced.

"Do not fret. I did not do your chores," Tante Klegg said. "When I released your Karl, he had the pail full and eggs tucked in his shirt."

Gretchen grinned at Karl, forgetting her embarrassment.

"Wasn't kicked or pecked once," he boasted.

Gretchen shared a smile until she realized Tante Klegg scrutinized them. "He's not my Karl," she said, gulping her milk.

Tante Klegg made a clucking noise and flicked her hand at Gretchen as if to call her silly. She pushed a plate at Karl and stood. "Do you want flapjacks?"

When he nodded, she retrieved a couple from the pan staying warm on the stove. This was the first solid food Karl had kept down since arriving on the farm eleven days ago.

Gretchen's frown deepened. "You should slow down," she warned. "You'll get sick if you keep eating that fast."

"Now that we *all* know that you are not John Wilkes Booth, there is no rush for you to leave." Tante Klegg dropped a dollop of batter onto the sizzling pan.

"Ma'am?" Karl said after choking for a moment.

Gretchen put her fork down. She was starting to feel like she was still dreaming.

"We, well, Gretchen needs help around the farm. I spend my hours tending to the farmhouse."

"Mama will never stand for it," Gretchen said.

"You have always been free to leave," Tante Klegg said to Karl, ignoring Gretchen. "But why would you? We are the only people you know."

Karl snorted. "Hardly could have left tied to a chair," he said.

Tante Klegg dropped a large flapjack on his plate. "Eat."

"Don't seem right," Karl mused. "Leaving good cooking for an unknown fate." He grabbed a forkful. "Besides, someone's gotta make sure y'all don't kill each other before Werner comes home, right?"

"Why are you two being nice to each other?" Gretchen said.

"Your ma, I mean, your aunt, came back from her walk this morning saying Alina's going to visit, and she's bringing her preacher pa," Karl said.

Tante Klegg nodded. "We must maintain our roles for Alina and Pastor Baumbach. I am your aunt. He is your *verlobter*. Tante Miller is your mother."

Adelaide swept into the room before Gretchen could protest. "This place is filthy," she said. "Are we to entertain guests with the house in such a state?"

"You can't be serious," Gretchen said. She pushed away her food, appetite lost. "You're worried about appearances with Alina? The one you said could only set foot in the house if Werner himself dragged her here?"

Adelaide poured a deep saucer of steaming coffee and motioned at Tante Klegg. "Your daughter needs a lesson in manners." Adelaide tipped the saucer to her lips and giggled. "Your daughter. I thought I would never say those words."

Gretchen's gaze dropped to her lap. Adelaide's cattiness should not have surprised her, but it did, and it hurt. "Don't you care for me at all?"

Adelaide set her saucer on the table and took Gretchen's chin in her fingers. "You were a distraction from my Werner." She sat as graceful as a petal. "If situations were different, I could have learned to love you. Your enthusiasm has a charm. But when you pushed that boy into the trough and gave Werner the opportunity to volunteer and then on the day our president dies, you adopt a damn Confederate!"

"I'm not a pet," Karl interrupted.

"No one asked you," Adelaide said.

Tante Klegg slammed the pan on the stove. "That is enough." She pointed at her sister. "Stop taking your bitterness out on the child. If you must be nasty, direct it at me."

"I'm not a child," Gretchen said.

"You cannot have it both ways," Adelaide said to Gretchen. "You are an adult, and you are ready to handle the consequences of your actions. Or you are a child, and someone else will speak for you."

Gretchen started laughing.

Adelaide rose from her chair, wringing her hands together. "I knew this would not end well."

"Oh?" Gretchen said between guffaws, "You knew? I wonder why? Because everything you've ever told me is a lie?"

"She's in shock," Karl said. "We saw it at the camp all the time. Someone would crack, and they'd be touched ever since."

"I'm not touched," Gretchen retorted. "You don't think this is funny? My aunt wants to be my mother, and my mother can't wait to be my aunt, and I don't want anything to do with either of them. I can't believe Alina wants to marry into this family. She has no idea what she's agreeing to!"

Tante Klegg put up her hand. "You should not speak to your—"

"My what?" Gretchen said. "Am I supposed to respect either of you after what you've done?"

"You are not supposed to *do* anything," Tante Klegg said. "You have heard our words. You may do as you like."

Gretchen pointed at her, finger shaking. "Don't you dare treat me like I'm an adult now."

The sounds of steps on the front porch prevented Tante Klegg from responding. Alina and her father had arrived.

No one expected the deep voice instead of Alina's usual greeting. "*Mütter*, I'm home."

TWENTY-TWO

Wednesday, 26 April 1865 / Grove City, Ohio

Everyone stared at one another. They could not look at who spoke for fear he was a figment of their collective imagination.

Werner slumped against the doorway, panting. Werner was home, unchanged and yet so changed. His dark hair and gaunt cheeks matched Karl's; his crazed expression did not.

Gretchen blinked, which was all it took for Adelaide to leap across the kitchen.

Werner watched with wide and bright eyes as his mother approached. He did not move, yet he seemed ready to pounce. Gretchen remembered seeing a wild dog watch a chicken the same way before snapping its neck. "Mama!" she warned, holding out her hand.

Adelaide slowed at Gretchen's call, but still she advanced.

"*Mütter?*" Werner whispered. He stared at his mother as if he had never seen her before.

Something was not right. Gretchen pushed Karl behind her, her annoyance with him forgotten. This was not the time for Werner to discover a Confederate in his home. Not when he looked like that.

"I deserted," Werner said to everyone and to no one. He spoke at his mother, but looked through her to Gretchen standing behind her. "That damned man; I deserted."

Gretchen gripped the back of the chair until her knuckles were white. Desertion was for cowards and traitors, not for her brother—that is, cousin—the Union hero.

"What man?" Adelaide asked, now backing away.

"That Lincoln," Werner said, his voice rising. "He made a speech saying the war wasn't about the Union at all. He said it was about slavery. He changed his mind about why we were dying and didn't tell us until it was too late for us to do anything about it! I went to war to save the Union, to stop the Confederacy, not to end slavery!"

Gretchen could not believe what she heard. "The Confederate states *are* slave states," she shouted. "What's the difference?"

"How could you have deserted?" Tante Klegg said.

"Where have you been?" Adelaide cried.

Werner rubbed his collarbone with his left hand, revealing his strawberry-shaped birthmark. Such a familiar, endearing move that reminded Gretchen of her father so much it hurt. She hoped her father had not deserted as well. She hoped he had done his duty to fight for the Union.

"Been running for two years," Werner said. He remained slumped, so Gretchen could not see why he hid his right hand. "Been running and getting shot at and running some more. Finally made it home in time to hear the president's gone, that fool. If he'd never made it about slavery... And what do we have in his place? You wait and see how Johnson's going to be president. The man's from Tennessee!"

Gretchen fought against Karl's grip on her arm. "Don't you talk about Mr. Lincoln that way. His plan was to bring the states back together! Johnson has to honor it!"

Werner's laugh was hollow. He slid down the doorjamb until he sat on the little landing outside of the kitchen. "Idealist," he threw at Gretchen, as if it were the worst thing in the world.

A muscle in Gretchen's cheek twitched. Karl's grip on her tightened, but she did not move.

Footsteps approached, and Alina's swaying skirts came into view. She knelt beside Werner and whispered into his ear. After Werner nodded, Alina drew his arm around her shoulders and helped him stand.

"*Mütter*," Alina said, "our Werner returned. Aren't you happy? Why's everyone shouting?"

Werner pulled away from Alina and walked into the room with a sway to his body. Each step threw him off balance. Watching him was like watching a cracked bell swinging in the church steeple: graceful, silent, and broken.

Adelaide shrieked. "What have they done to you?"

Werner stumbled. Alina rushed forward to catch him and together they righted themselves. Tante Klegg, Adelaide, Gretchen, and Karl could only stare.

Werner relied on Alina's arm with the one he had left. An empty sleeve hung limp from his other shoulder, pinned shut where his elbow should have been. Now that he was out of the harsh morning sunlight, Gretchen could see Werner's face. He looked... skeletal. He was far worse than Karl had been when he had fallen at her feet in the garden.

Alina's face was pale, almost white. It took Gretchen a moment to realize she wore powder to hide a bruised jaw. A smug sense of satisfaction washed over her.

"I went to war, Ma, not choir practice," Werner said, glancing at Alina.

Alina's pinched smile made Gretchen want to vomit.

How like Werner. It was not enough to come home; he had to bring Alina with him. It was not enough to say, "Ma, I'm home"; he had to make them all sound like crazed and ignorant women.

And if they all were a little crazy, who could blame them? What else could they do, trapped on the home front, waiting to hear the worst and knowing they could do nothing?

"Your arm." His mother faltered. "My baby." She began to cry. Not the loud nonsense she was so fond of, more theatrics than emotion. Large tears rolled down her pale cheeks. She did not bother wiping them away. She just stood there, silent and staring and crying.

Nothing ever happened as it should. Werner fought for the Union and should have returned a hero, if only because he survived. He was not supposed to be a nasty traitor, a deserter to the cause he left to fight for.

"What *were* you yelling about?" Werner asked. "Wasn't exactly the homecoming I was expecting, *ja?*"

"Got a notion they were yelling about me," Karl said.

Gretchen whipped around. *No, no, no.*

Before anyone could blink, Werner had a revolver pulled and pointed at Karl's stomach. "Who are you?"

"This is Gretchen's *verlobter,*" Alina said.

"Her what?" Werner shouted.

Alina shrank back. "You didn't get my letter?"

"You don't get letters when you're in hiding!" Werner said.

Gretchen stared at the man who, for all intents, was her brother. Her aunt and mother had raised Werner as her brother, anyway. The similarities between his face and her own still struck her as if they twins. Memories overwhelmed her. He used to lock her in the cellar until she cried herself to sleep. He used to kick her lunch pail out of sight and make her late for school. The lashings she would receive. That he snickered when his mother scolded Gretchen for daring to catch pneumonia.

Gretchen realized Werner was a terrible brother. She did not care what he had gone through. He was a spoiled, hateful person, and the war had not changed him for the better.

"What happened to Joshua?" Werner asked. "Wasn't she pining after him? Or did she forget him that fast?" He focused on Karl. The hand holding the revolver did not waiver, though his balance did.

"*Liebchen*, you must sit," his mother said, gesturing at a chair.

Werner ignored her. He cocked the revolver. "What happened to Joshua?"

"Who's Joshua?" Karl asked, frowning at Gretchen.

"Joshua was the most handsome boy in the school room," Alina explained. She hovered behind Werner. "And he was not German. Like you." She crossed her arms and popped her hip. "He was smart. Gretchen followed him everywhere, but especially when Werner and I began courting."

"Don't be stupid," Gretchen said. "I did no such thing. And Werner, point that thing at the ground. You'll hurt someone!"

"Don't you think that's the point?" Karl whispered.

"One day," Alina continued as if Gretchen and Karl had not spoken, "Joshua told Gretchen for everyone to hear that she was an unkempt child. That she would do better to learn how to braid her hair and take care of a garden than to best him in class like a boy. He humiliated her, and me, too."

"Because everything is about you," Gretchen said.

"I was going to marry into a family with this stubborn girl who had nothing better to do than follow a non-German boy around!" Alina continued. "And what was Gretchen's response? She shoved him into a horse trough, as if that would change his mind about her."

"That was the day Werner volunteered," his mother said, glaring at Gretchen. The old wound was fresh again.

"Yes," Alina said. She wrapped her arm around Werner's waist, careful not to jar him. "Gretchen and Joshua distracted everyone, and Werner enlisted to secure our future."

Gretchen's gaze dropped. That was why Werner went to war. Not to save the Union or stop the Confederacy or even to stop the enslavement of an entire people.

"The army promised to pay well," Alina crooned. "Werner could afford his own farm sooner than if he worked for his father."

Gretchen's breath caught in her throat. Werner went to war because he was greedy. He did not want to wait to inherit the farm from their father. He went to war for money. He was no better than those Confederate blockade runners they read about in the papers. He intended to profit from the deaths of others.

"Then... what did happen to Joshua?" Karl asked.

"He got exactly what he deserved," Gretchen said. "He revealed he was a bully. He wanted to show his strength. He went to war to prove he was a man."

Karl shook his head. "Prove he is a man" echoed over and over in his head. He hardly heard Gretchen say Joshua died in his first battle. Instead, Karl heard his own voice whispering, "Gotta prove I am a man. Gotta prove I am a man. *Gonna* prove I am a man. In my way." Karl fell back, missing the chair behind him and crashing to the floor.

Werner shouted not to move, or he would shoot.

Tante Klegg slapped the revolver from Werner's hand. She told him to sit down and shut his mouth before he caused any more trouble.

Adelaide shrieked at Tante Klegg not to lay another hand on her boy.

A roaring, whooshing noise filled Karl's ears. He clutched his head. He gasped. He remembered.

He remembered someone shouting at him. Someone wanted him to stand up, to take notice of the world. His father. His mother had cried. She had light hair, unlike his. His brother had looked on in disgust, already in his Confederate grays. And there Karl had stood, clutching a box with a curtain, not being a man, but on his way to getting there.

"Karl," Gretchen said, grabbing his shoulders, "what's wrong?"

"What was in the box?" Karl asked before slumping out of consciousness.

TWENTY-THREE

Wednesday, 26 April 1865 / Grove City, Ohio

Karl woke to the deep murmurs of a masculine voice. He froze, expecting to struggle against bound hands and feet now that Werner had returned. Instead, someone had tucked him into bed. A large hand rested on his shoulder.

The voice paused, sensing Karl's stirring. When Karl pretended to be asleep, the familiar voice resumed in a language Karl did not recognize. And then, startling Karl, the man said in his heavy accent, "I know that you are awake. You have nothing to fear. You may open your eyes."

Karl cleared his throat. He peeked to find the bearded pastor from Gretchen's church watching him with a conspiring grin. He looked around, surprised he was back in Werner's bedroom. He did not know how that had happened now that the prodigal son had returned. Karl did not like how the pastor had tied the door handle to his chair so no one could get inside.

"What were you saying?" Karl asked as he sat up.

"I asked *mein Gott* to keep watch over His child. To guide you to your rightful mind."

Karl rubbed his shoulder, which ached from where he had landed. "Kind of you."

Pastor Baumbach shook his head, grin fading. "It is kind to Gretchen and to my Alina who will marry Gretchen's brother." He leaned back in the chair, and it groaned under his weight. He clasped his hands on his healthy belly.

Karl wondered how many meals at home with family, away from bullets and screams, created that belly.

"Fräulein Klegg continues to say you are to wed Gretchen," Pastor Baumbach said.

Karl wished he had not said anything. Even without remembering a lot about his father, he could tell a lecture was about to happen. "That's what I hear, too."

"You do not want to marry Gretchen?" Pastor Baumbach said.

Karl shrugged. He realized that was a mistake when Pastor Baumbach's expression darkened. "That's not it..."

Annoyance wafted off Pastor Baumbach. Karl felt the room grow warmer.

"Things moved fast," Karl said.

"How fast?" Pastor Baumbach asked. His tone was careful, ready to disapprove.

Karl did not know what to say. He did not know how much Pastor Baumbach knew, since Gretchen claimed she could not lie to him. Not that Karl wanted to talk about Gretchen anyway. And he for certain did not want a father-son chat with Pastor Baumbach about her.

Karl sighed. He was trapped with a religious man staring him down. He could see Pastor Baumbach waiting to accuse him of seducing Gretchen. Karl figured if that were the case, then the bright side was he must look stronger than a week ago when Gretchen found him.

Pastor Baumbach's expression continued to darken until it looked like he was fit to burst.

Karl scowled. He could hardly say, "Who cares about Gretchen? I remembered something about myself. Will you let me be so I can remember more?"

All Karl wanted to think about was that memory. Something about a box with a curtain. It must have been the last time he saw his family.

"I do not know a great deal about you," Pastor Baumbach said. "I do not know what you mean by saying things went fast."

His emphasis on the last word made Karl's face burn. "Why do all you Dutchmen think I'm only around to take advantage of Gretchen? First Tante Klegg, now you! I no more chose this farm than it chose me! When a man's on death's door, he don't get to choose which door to walk through."

Pastor Baumbach leapt to his feet. "What did you call us?" he roared.

Karl's mouth dropped open. He shrank back under Pastor Baumbach's towering rage. He tried to remember what he had said.

"Where did you hear such a word?" Pastor Baumbach demanded.

Karl shook his head, shrinking further away.

"*Dutchmen*," Pastor Baumbach said. "I hate to have to say it."

Karl had no idea where that word came from, but it seemed it was a terrible thing to say. That was the thing about not having a memory. Karl had no idea what other words would come out at the worst time.

Someone pounded on the bedroom door. "What's wrong?" Gretchen said.

Pastor Baumbach sat down, glaring at Karl. He called over his shoulder, "Nothing, Fräulein Gretchen. Tend to your brother."

"He doesn't need me," Gretchen scoffed, "he's got Alina. What's going on in there?"

Karl held his palms up and met Pastor Baumbach's gaze. "I'm sorry," he said, striving for sincerity. "I don't know where that came from."

Pastor Baumbach's jaw worked. After a tense moment of listening to Gretchen pace outside the door, he ran his fingers through his beard. "I can see that."

Karl began to play with the coverlet on his lap. He had a feeling this conversation was not going to improve.

"I worry you have so much in that head of yours that could hurt Gretchen and you would have no idea."

Karl chuckled. "Unlikely."

"Oh?"

"Well, Gretchen lets everyone know when she's upset. If I said something stupid, wouldn't take long for you, or anyone else, to know."

"This is true," Pastor Baumbach admitted.

"And she's an excellent shot. If I mess up, she'll take care of me."

Pastor Baumbach's expression shifted. "But will you take care of her?"

"No one takes care of Gretchen. They just don't get in her way."

"You are insightful for a man without a mind," Pastor Baumbach mused.

Karl bristled. "I got a mind. I don't got a memory." He scratched at the bandage wrapped around his head. "And I could take care of her, if she'd let me. I learn fast, and I'd treat her right, because she's treated me right. I owe her my life."

Pastor Baumbach's eyebrows rose.

"Actually, I'm glad I owe her my life," Karl said, more to himself than to Pastor Baumbach. "She's got a good heart, and she's loyal, and fierce. Could do much worse. These days, people are your friends until you realize they're your enemy."

"What are you talking about in there?" Gretchen said through the door.

"Will you get out of here? I'm chatting with the pastor," Karl shouted.

After a stunned moment of silence, Gretchen made a loud huffing noise and stomped out of the house.

Pastor Baumbach stared at Karl with appreciation. "Perhaps Tante Klegg was right to choose you."

Karl kicked away the coverlet and dropped his feet to the floor. He leaned closer to Pastor Baumbach. "Why? Because I yelled at her?"

Pastor Baumbach frowned. "No, because she listened to you. Gretchen is headstrong and smart. She would not listen to you if she did not respect you."

Karl leaned back, surprised and pleased with his answer.

"Though," Pastor Baumbach continued, stroking his beard, "how she can respect a man who has no memory of who he is.... That is beyond me."

"And here I thought we could get along, Pastor."

Pastor Baumbach tented his fingers together. "Are you aware of how we Lutherans prepare for marriage?"

Karl shook his head. "Gretchen didn't say anything and believe it or not, I do remember everything that's happened since I got here."

"And how did you come to be on the Miller farm?"

Karl wished he had not sent Gretchen away. He began to suspect why she could never lie to Pastor Baumbach. His eyes, so blue, made him seem innocent. Being a holy man heightened the effect.

"Got left behind," Karl said.

Pastor Baumbach scratched his cheek. "Left behind? I recall you arrived as we learned about the president."

Karl ran his hand down his face. "Is this all you Yankees do? See conspiracy theories and blame the first stranger with an accent?"

Pastor Baumbach shrugged. "Perhaps we are still at war with our president taken from us."

"Well, I'm not," Karl said. "Why's it so difficult to understand I only want to know who I am, and where I come from, and if my family will have me back?"

"And what if you learn you were better not knowing these things?" Pastor Baumbach asked, more curious than judgmental.

"Don't think that's going to happen," Karl said. "I know I had a ma, and a pa, and a brother, and I want to know what happened to them."

With a little squeal, Gretchen fell into the bedroom. She held a knife in her hand from where she had cut her way through the rope locking the door shut. "Anyone interested in coffee?"

TWENTY-FOUR

Wednesday, 26 April 1865 / Grove City, Ohio

Gretchen rushed to hide her ankles. She could tell by Karl's set shoulders and tightness around his eyes that he was not happy she was there. He had no call for displeasure. She was here to save him from Pastor Baumbach's interrogation... by starting one of her own.

"*Guten tag*, Gretchen," Pastor Baumbach said. He sat at the foot of the bed and waved for Gretchen to take his chair. "Did you worry I was telling your *verlobter* the family secrets?"

Gretchen snorted and clapped her hand over her mouth.

Pastor Baumbach patted the chair. "Come. Join our conversation. We were about to speak of wedding preparations."

Gretchen laid the knife by the wall and patted it, as if she would return to it later. "It sounded like you were distracting Karl from remembering his past." She sat in the chair, placed her hands in her lap, and smiled at Pastor Baumbach. "But I'm not here to talk about Karl. I'd like to let Karl rest for a moment. He's had a rough week."

Pastor Baumbach frowned, seeming confused. Gretchen was glad.

She swallowed and said in as calm and collected voice as she could manage, "Why did Werner go to your farm before ours?"

Karl slouched against the headboard. It was obvious he would not be alone for a while yet, so he might as well get comfortable. He stretched his legs out, but kept his feet from Pastor Baumbach sitting on the end of the bed.

Pastor Baumbach shifted in his chair. "Have you asked your brother this question?"

Gretchen's jaw worked. Werner was no more her brother than Karl was. She could not tell Pastor Baumbach that, though. Not until Werner married Alina. Even after all the cruel things Werner had said and done to her, Gretchen did not hate her cousin. She did not understand Werner, but she did not like him, either.

Pastor Baumbach folded his hands over his round belly.

"I tried," Gretchen admitted, "but he refused to answer and then Alina and Tan—" she paused. She licked her lips and tried again. "Mama sent me away because I was upsetting Werner."

"Yes," Pastor Baumbach said, nodding. "Werner has always been excitable."

"That's one way to put it," Gretchen said. "You could also say he's prone to tantrums."

Having been on the receiving end of Werner's trigger hand, Karl thought this was an understatement.

"He went to your farm because he was so upset that he couldn't even come home?" Gretchen asked.

Pastor Baumbach cleared his throat. "I should not say if it will upset Werner."

"This is the same boy who proposed to your daughter behind your back and then ran off to war," Gretchen said. "He's not a saint because he lost an arm."

Pastor Baumbach ran his hand down his face. "How large your mind must be. You never forget moments that, if you did forget them, would make you a happier person. You are so like your aunt. Do you know this?"

"You're stalling," Gretchen said.

Karl thought Gretchen was channeling her anger well. That was twice now that Pastor Baumbach had referenced her family. That was twice that she had not taken the bait. How long until Gretchen admitted her brother was her cousin and her aunt was her mother?

"Werner came to us last Sunday, after Alina returned from her visit with you after church." Pastor Baumbach's expression was wry. "After you bruised her face and made her almost unrecognizable to her own *verlobter*."

Gretchen flushed.

"I know my daughter, and I know you," Pastor Baumbach said. "I must assume she said something that made you lose your patience."

Gretchen held up her hand. "And if I did?"

Pastor Baumbach shrugged. "My daughter takes after my wife. Which is to say, they live in their own interpretation of the world. They do not like it when someone reminds them. And if I were honest, I would say I am surprised it did not happen sooner."

Gretchen sat there, not expecting to hear such things from the pastor about his own wife and child. She wondered whether the world was falling to pieces around her, or if she was waking to the reality of the world.

Pastor Baumbach turned to Karl, whose entire body flinched under the attention. "You study me. You are uncertain whether to call me friend or enemy."

"A sign one way or the other would help," Karl said. "Can't tell if you're here to help me or Gretchen or anyone else. I thank you for your prayers, though."

"There is only one enemy, and that is the enemy of the Lord," Pastor Baumbach said.

Karl laced his fingers behind his head and crossed his ankles together. "When I was in... the war, I heard men on both sides saying the Lord was on their side. Were they lying?"

Pastor Baumbach shook his head. "The Lord is with everyone who needs Him."

"Well, I guess Werner needs Him pretty bad if he can't remember where his family is," Gretchen said. She flinched when Pastor Baumbach glared at her, but then she waved her hand at him. "I know, I know. Werner's seen all sorts of things in the war, and I need to give him time. But guess what? Werner's been out of the war a long time. He's been hiding because he's a deserter."

Gretchen slapped the mattress. "Why did he even desert? Who's going to keep a soldier with one arm? Excitable, that's what we keep calling him. All I see is plain selfishness, and I'm tired of everyone defending him."

"Gretchen," Pastor Baumbach interrupted, "what is wrong? This is not like you."

Hands clenching into fists, Gretchen stood. "I was wrong to come in here," she said. "And you're right, this isn't like me. This is, however, the most I've ever acted like Werner's sibling, which is funny, considering."

"You act as though he betrayed you by reaching my farm first," Pastor Baumbach said, wonder in his voice. "He was feverish, he thought he was home, and it took days for his fever to break. We could not move him until he was out of harm's way. Did you not notice Alina's visits had stopped? She was his nursemaid all that time."

Gretchen shook her head. She had not noticed Alina's absence. She had been worrying Karl was the president's murderer. She had been waiting for signs that Karl's memory was returning. She had suffered the shock of learning she was her aunt's daughter.

Also, Gretchen had assumed Alina knew she was not welcome at the farm until Werner returned. Now that Werner had returned, everything was different now. Gretchen no longer cared what Werner and Alina did. She did care what Karl knew about his past.

Pastor Baumbach rested his elbows on his knees and clasped his hands together. "I do not know what is happening with this family. I hope Werner and Alina's wedding will begin the process of healing." When neither spoke, Pastor Baumbach shook his head and left the room.

After a few moments, they heard voices and feet shuffling. The kitchen door shut behind Werner, Alina, and Pastor Baumbach. Adelaide began to cry. Tante Klegg's heavier footsteps paced in the kitchen before storming out of the house.

"Is that bad?" Karl whispered.

"Well, it can't be good," Gretchen retorted.

BOOTH KILLED AND HEROLD CAPTURED

Friday, 28 April 1865 / The Ohio Daily Statesman

It will rejoice the people, as it does us, to learn that Booth, the man who assassinated President Lincoln, has been killed.

Perhaps the gratification would be greater if Booth had been taken alive; but this he evidently had determined should not be done. The particulars attending his death and of the capture of his accomplice Herold, will be found in the telegraphic columns.

Booth was shot, and survived three or four hours. In the first dispatch announcing the circumstances attending his attempted capture and death, we were told that he died blaspheming the Government. In the later dispatch this statement is not repeated, but it is reported that when asked if he had anything to say, he replied: "Tell my mother I died for my country."

This message suggests the question; "How did he suppose his country would be served in the assassination of President Lincoln?"

The man Herold, who has been captured alive, may throw some light on this subject or he may not. As Booth was on the threshold of eternity, he did not even utter one word of contrition for the infamous crime he had perpetrated.

162

TWENTY-FIVE

Friday, 28 April 1865 / Grove City, Ohio

Gretchen listened to the familiar words of Werner and Alina's ceremony, but paid them no mind. She stood in Pastor Baumbach's home as a witness with her mother, aunt, Mrs. Baumbach, and Karl. Pastor Baumbach kept glancing at Gretchen, searching and concerned. She paid him no mind, either.

She counted the number of flounces on Alina's dress instead. There were fifteen, and they ran the entire circumference of her skirt. Mrs. Baumbach sewed every last one of those flounces. Gretchen knew because Mrs. Baumbach had said so five times before the ceremony began.

Gretchen rolled her shoulder, trying to ease a pinch point on her rib cage where a bone from the corset poked her. Adelaide frowned at her to stop fidgeting.

Gretchen had watched Mrs. Baumbach and Adelaide fuss and flutter over Alina all morning. Now that Werner was back, his mother had been happy to forgive and accept Alina. Alina had to look perfect for Werner, of course. Gretchen had fought her hand-me-down corset and hoops until Tante Klegg had arrived. She had stopped Gretchen from strangling herself by her own sleeve.

"Remind me why I have to wear this stuff?" Gretchen had said between clenched teeth.

"You must dress your age now," had been Tante Klegg's reply.

Werner and Alina began reciting their vows. Alina cried, and Werner's collar seemed too tight.

It had taken Adelaide all night to get all the grime out of Werner's uniform. He stood in his tattered blues, sleeve pinned up to hide his missing arm. He looked nervous and excited and tired and annoyed.

Gretchen glanced at Karl, who looked uncomfortable wearing Werner's old Sunday best. She lacked time to fit the suit to him, so she did as best she could. Only a few stitches tacked the pant hem and sleeve cuffs so Karl did not swim in fabric.

Pastor Baumbach described Alina's unwavering patience while waiting for Werner's return. He mentioned Werner's perseverance to return to his bride.

Gretchen stared at her feet so no one would see her rolling her eyes.

The newspapers that morning had announced authorities had caught Booth and his conspirators. Her aunt and mother had continued eating breakfast as if the almanac reported a sunny day.

It was for the best. At least, Gretchen kept telling herself that. They had lost interest in Mr. Lincoln's killer. They had also lost interest in Karl. Karl was Gretchen's problem in the full definition of the word. Pastor Baumbach had intended a double ceremony that morning, but Tante Klegg had stopped it.

It did not make a lick of sense since Gretchen was certain Pastor Baumbach thought she was fifteen. How could he marry her off to a stranger and have a clear conscience?

Karl, sensing Gretchen was watching him, gave her a small smile. She did not return it.

Tomorrow they were going to Columbus. She did not know what that would mean for Karl or for her. The newspaper had shared the agenda for Mr. Lincoln's funeral train's arrival at the statehouse. Everyone in the region would travel to the capital city to pay their respects.

All Alina heard was Mr. Lincoln's funeral would distract everyone. That meant no wait to walk into a photographer's shop so she could get her wedding photo.

So they were going to Columbus tomorrow, Karl too, because it seemed foolhardy to leave him alone. Gretchen wondered whether anyone would recognize him as the lost prisoner. She wondered if, like her mother and aunt, no one cared anymore with the president's body within reach.

Pastor Baumbach pronounced Werner and Alina as man and wife. They kissed. Alina threw her arms around Werner's neck, saying, "We must never part."

Werner looked sick to his stomach before burying his face in her neck.

Gretchen felt a little sad. Alina would have the rest of her life getting to know this man she had married. She did not like Alina, but she also did not like the idea of her suffering. How Gretchen hoped Werner would be a kinder husband than he was a brother.

Werner wrapped his arm around Alina's waist, already the possessive husband. "Though I'm still angry at Mr. Lincoln," he said, "I'm glad our wedding gives us cause to pay our respects to him."

Gretchen rolled her eyes. She would have found a way to Columbus with or without Werner's wedding. This was her chance to see Mr. Lincoln in person. This was also her chance to see if her father—well, her uncle—was on any lists. It had been weeks since they had heard anything. With Karl there and Werner home, it had been easy to ignore the fact that no one knew what had happened to Gregory Miller.

Until this wedding. Gretchen's father should have been here for the wedding. One way or another, she had to know if he was on any lists: the prisoners of war, the missing, or the deceased.

Werner broke Gretchen's reverie. "Out of respect for our former president, I'm allowing this so-called Karl to remain on my farm until Monday."

Gretchen's mouth dropped open. "Your farm?" She stepped closer. "Your farm?" she shouted.

"Gretchen," Tante Klegg warned.

"Who said it was your farm?" Gretchen demanded. "I've been watching over the farm since Papa left, not you. This is more my farm than it ever was yours. You left!"

Tante Klegg clucked her tongue at Gretchen and shook her head. She gave her a well-meaning look with a pained smile. Gretchen's hand came to her mouth as she realized she had no claim to the farm because she was not the daughter of the family.

Werner made it clear he knew exactly what Gretchen was thinking. "I know Mr. Lincoln wanted reconciliation. But I bet he also wanted to live. Just like how I want my arm back."

Pastor Baumbach frowned and shut his Bible. Adelaide wiped tears from her cheeks. Tante Klegg was impassive, and Karl was white as a sheet.

"I'm man of the house, Gretchen," Werner said. "And don't you think I know how Karl got into my house?"

Gretchen took a step back, shaking her head.

Werner continued, "You and your mother are no longer welcome. When your pet Karl leaves, so will you."

"You would evict us?" Tante Klegg said.

Pastor Baumbach held up his hand. "We should not have pushed for this so soon, Alina. It was unwise. It was selfish of us in his state."

Alina ignored her father. She looked from Tante Klegg to Gretchen, clutching Werner's hand at her waist. "Gretchen is your daughter?"

The room fell silent.

Pastor Baumbach hugged his Bible to his chest and regarded Gretchen. "This is what upset you. Not Werner's return."

Gretchen, her throat closing with tears, could say nothing.

Pastor Baumbach gave a measured look to everyone in the room, Tante Klegg and Adelaide in particular. He retreated to his bedroom.

Still pondering, Alina said, "You're not his sister at all."

Gretchen lifted her chin.

"I'm serious," Werner said, guiding Alina to the kitchen. "I want the three of you out by Monday or so help me, I'll shoot every last one of you."

Mrs. Baumbach and Adelaide did not look at Tante Klegg, Gretchen, or Karl when they followed Werner and Alina into the kitchen.

"Now do you see why I kept your lineage a secret?" Tante Klegg said. She lifted her skirts and sailed out of the house. Moments later, Gretchen and Karl heard the wagon creaking down the road.

Gretchen's shoulders drooped. "I guess we're walking home."

ROUTE OF FUNERAL PROCESSION

Saturday, 29 April 1865 / The Ohio Daily Statesman

MILITARY PREPARATIONS *in this city for the Funeral Ceremonies of the late Abraham Lincoln, President of the United States, who Died at Washington by the Hands of an Assassin, on the 15th day of April, 1865.*

1. *The remains of Abraham Lincoln, late president of the United States, will arrive in the city of Columbus, O., at 7:30 o'clock A.M. Saturday, the 29th inst., at the Union Depot.*
2. *The funeral escort will consist of the 88th O.V. Infantry.*

III. *Officers of the army not on duty with troops are respectfully invited to participate in the obsequies.*

1. *Detachments of the army and volunteer organizations, not on duty with the escort, will be assigned positions on application to Capt. L. Nichols, Tod Barracks.*
2. *All military officers to be in uniform and with side arms. The usual badge of mourning will be worn on the left arm and sword hilt.*
3. *In order to prevent confusion at the entrance gate, all who are not*

in line of procession, will form after the left of the procession has entered the Capitol square, in two ranks on the outside of square fence, on High street, running North to Broad, South to State, thence East on Broad and State streets, for extent.

ROUTE OF PROCESSION. *The procession will move promptly from south of depot at 7:30 A.M. South on High to Broad, east on Broad to Fourth, South on Fourth to State, west on State to High, north on High to main entrance of Capitol. A mounted cavalry force will be stationed at all intersections of High street north of Town street, for the purpose of preventing all vehicles from entering on High street. That street must be kept clear for the movement of the procession. At 6 P.M. the Capitol will be closed. The procession will reform in the following order to escort the remains to the depot...*

TWENTY-SIX

Saturday, 29 April 1865 / Columbus, Ohio

Gretchen avoided bumping shoulders with Tante Klegg and Karl, who had kept her up late by speaking into the small hours of the night. Her eyes were bleary, and her head and heart heavy. Her entire body trembled from exhaustion. She did her best not to yawn as the wagon swayed.

Adelaide had slept at the Baumbach's, preferring to travel with her son and new daughter-in-law to Columbus to pay her respects to Mr. Lincoln.

Gretchen had never visited the capital city. She was sad and excited to pay her respects to Mr. Lincoln. And scared, if she had to admit it, because there was a chance that her father's name would be on a list. She hoped he was on a list of soldiers sent to Camp Chase for mustering out. Or on a hospital list. Or even on a missing persons list.

Gretchen dreaded finding his name on any other list.

Karl's hand brushed hers when the wagon bounced over a rut in the road. Both jumped. Gretchen clasped both of her hands together in her lap so it would not happen again. When she glanced at Karl from under the brim of her bonnet, he was as bright as a ripe tomato.

Gretchen looked at Tante Klegg, who had not noticed or chose not to notice. Tante Klegg had not said a word to her all morning. It was obvious she blamed Gretchen for getting them kicked out of the farmhouse.

The thing was, Gretchen suspected that had been Werner's plan all along. That his mother went along with Werner without arguing seemed to confirm it. One way or another, those two had planned to get Gretchen and Tante Klegg out, and Karl was the perfect excuse.

"Them cussed fools," Gretchen said to herself.

They neared the city; wagons and buggies lined the road for miles ahead. Tante Klegg pulled the horse aside and tethered the reins to a tree. "We will walk from here. We cannot get our wagon through this mess."

The crowds were unfathomable. People filled muddy streets, lined boardwalks, and waved handkerchiefs out of windows. Tante Klegg, Karl, and Gretchen shuffled into the line to view the president's remains. Black crepe fabric wound around the state-house's tall columns so they looked like striped candy.

Most faces wore expressions of shock, dismay, or a certain weary acceptance. Some displayed something more sinister. Grim satis-faction—that was how Gretchen would have described them. She wanted to scream at them for daring to view Mr. Lincoln. They were gloating; that is what they were doing. They were happy Booth took someone so important to the Union. Gretchen felt like she kept seeing Werner's smirk everywhere. She balled her fists together.

The man beside Gretchen shoved her with his elbow. She cried out as she stumbled into Karl. The man ignored her, shoving his way to the front of the line.

"All right?" Karl said, helping Gretchen stand. She nodded and looked away from Tante Klegg's raised eyebrows and pressed lips.

They shuffled forward. Gretchen could feel her heart beat against her corset. She wished she had grabbed an apple before they climbed into the wagon that morning.

A woman said something about finally seeing the president's comeuppance. Someone else shushed her and said she should not speak ill of the dead.

Gretchen shuddered. She wondered whether anyone was cruel enough to do further harm to Mr. Lincoln. She had read his casket would be open for the mourners to view. She had heard there was a man whose sole purpose was to apply chalk and paint to Mr. Lincoln's face to hide the decay.

They reached the official mourning line sometime after noon. The line circled the statehouse block and beyond. Gretchen knew they had until six, when the funeral train would leave for Indianapolis.

Tante Klegg maintained her silence as they waited. Gretchen shifted from side to side, craning her neck to guess how long it would take to reach the doors. Karl did not know how to feel or act. He remembered, in part, swearing citizenship to the United States when he left Camp Chase. By default, Mr. Lincoln was the only president he knew. Had he been a stalwart Confederate before capture and fever and memory loss? He had no idea. Tante Klegg had pestered him with questions late into the night. His head still swam from trying to remember, trying to appease her.

Their conversation had not been easy. Tante Klegg wanted to know why he was in Camp Chase. In the early morning hours, she had convinced herself that she and Gretchen had to leave, and he as well. "You must join us," she had said, "or you must disappear. You will not survive Werner."

Karl wanted to ask Gretchen whether she knew Tante Klegg had given him the opportunity to leave. That if he remained, he had to marry her.

Gretchen clutched Karl's hand as the crowd pushed them to the side. She complained about the crowd's changing mood. They stumbled trying to match the crowd's pace. A flash caught Karl's eye.

At the edge of the crowd stood a man with a delicate contraption. Karl could not pull his gaze away. The contraption was a precarious box atop three spindly legs. The man standing behind it held up a thin stick with a smoking tray. Karl released Tante Klegg's hand without realizing it.

"Not now," Tante Klegg said as Karl inched through the crowd. He made sure to turn around and shake his head. He did not want her to think he was taking her offer. Not yet, anyway.

Karl pushed through, Gretchen following because he had not released her hand. The man lifted the heavy black fabric hanging off the back of the box. Karl froze. It was just like his memory. The man stepped underneath the fabric, draping it over his head and shoulders.

Tante Klegg moved farther away with the crowd. The doors were about to open so they could pay their respects to Mr. Lincoln. Gretchen's head swiveled from Tante Klegg to Karl, unsure who she should follow.

The man clicked a thin piece of wood in place at the front of the box. He emerged and pulled out a glass plate, which he encased in a thin wooden sleeve and tucked away in the box at his feet.

"What's that you're doing?" Karl asked.

"Capturing history," the man exclaimed. He pulled another pane of reflective glass and slid it into place.

"How long are you exposing for?" Karl asked, without knowing what he meant.

The man's brows arched but he spouted off words that made no sense until they did. Focus, light, and a steady stand were key to a good capture, Karl remembered. The subject must be still because the light took time to burn the treated glass. That was why stills of battles were no good. Better to capture the equipment, or the campground, or the bodies after a skirmish. Movement was impossible to capture.

Karl's heart was not in capturing details. It was too easy to make a mistake and waste expensive materials. Karl looked at his trembling hands. "Might I?"

The photographer stared at him. Gretchen clapped her hands over her mouth, her eyes bright with excitement. She moved onto the boardwalk to get out of the way of everyone pushing toward the statehouse. Tante Klegg, grumbling, did the same.

The photographer hovered as Karl lifted the velvet. The photographer rattled off instructions, but Karl did not listen; he did not need to. This contraption was not his profession, but it was his trade. He could, if he had to, step in and take the still if his partner fell to a bullet.

Karl stepped beneath the curtain. It felt like the most natural thing to happen since he left Camp Chase. He breathed a sigh as the velvet muffled the noises around him. All he had to do was concentrate. Find the scene. Slide open the front panel at the right moment. Hold up the flash. His assistant lights the fuse. Everyone holds still. Latch the panel shut again.

Karl blinked, and the statehouse disappeared. In front of him was a body. The face stared at him, unseeing. An arm outstretched on the ground, reaching for help that was too late coming. Of course, that was not where the body fell, no. Karl had moved the body. Made it a *real* scene. Needed to pull at the heartstrings back home. Rally everyone for the cause. What cause would warrant disturbing the body of a boy who died so he could take a good picture?

Karl stumbled away from the large camera. He fought the urge to retch all over himself.

The photographer leaped to prevent the camera from falling over. "Get out of here before you break something," he hissed.

Gretchen grabbed Karl's arm. "You know how to use that thing, don't you?"

Karl nodded. He bent at the waist and clutched his knees as he gulped foul-tasting air.

"You're a photographer?" Gretchen pressed, waving Tante Klegg over. They had to get out of there. They had to see the president. They had to find the list of the missing and the dead. They had to help Karl remember who he was. He was so close to remembering, she could tell.

Karl shook his head. He took a long, steadying breath and stood upright. "Photographer's assistant," he said.

Gretchen put her hand to her ear to show she had not heard him. The doors had opened at the statehouse. Everyone was rushing forward, hoping to make it through.

"Photographer's assistant," Karl said. "I can take them stills. I have taken them, after a bullet felled my employer. They almost got me. I was fumbling with the equipment. Trying to get out of the way. I didn't want to get shot. I was documenting history."

Gretchen's grip tightened. "You aren't a soldier."

He pressed the heels of his hands against his forehead. "I think... my name's... Elias."

"And my name's Witt," the photographer said, "and if you ruined my camera, so help me God..."

TWENTY-SEVEN

Saturday, 29 April 1865 / Columbus, Ohio

"I don't see it," Gretchen said. She spun on her heel to join a waving Tante Klegg. Their grouping was the next to enter the statehouse.

Karl jogged to catch up. "Don't see what? That's my name. You can't say you don't see it; it just is."

Gretchen's mouth was a thin line.

Tante Klegg snatched Gretchen and Karl by their shoulders, whipping them around. She would hear nothing about Karl's new-found memories. She refused to hear his name or how he took a photo with that stranger's equipment but almost knocked it over. She pushed them forward so they would not lose their place.

"Aren't you the least bit interested?" Gretchen said.

Tante Klegg glared at her. "We are not here to play detective, *liebchen*—"

"Stop calling me that."

"We are here to pay our respects to our president," Tante Klegg said. "Have you no shame?"

Tante Klegg was right. Gretchen needed to focus on mourning the president. She had left little time for mourning while trying to determine Karl's identity. And here Karl had discovered his identity without her help. Gretchen huffed. Some detective nursemaid she was.

Karl was silent as they approached the statehouse's west gate. An arch loomed overhead, inscribed with the words, "Ohio Mourns." Above the black striped columns hung a banner with a quote from Mr. Lincoln's last inaugural address: "With malice to no one. With charity for all."

It was a misquote. Mr. Lincoln's second inaugural speech had said, "With malice to none." None. Gretchen closed her eyes and inhaled.

So many thoughts jumbled around. Karl fought to make heads or tails of them. Some memories felt so clear, like seeing that boy's body, or watching his employer fall over dead. Others were hazy. He remembered the feel more than the look his mother gave him when he announced his intentions to become a war photographer. He would not fight for states that had never fought for them.

He was a Confederate photographer, but he was no more Confederate than Gretchen. With each step, he felt memories shuffle into place. His family had been farmers in Tennessee, but they were poor. They did not have slaves. They did not have money. His brother went to war to show that a poor farmer could shoot as well as a rich one.

A lot of good that did, since the Confederacy had lost. Those graybacks were not any good now.

"I don't understand why you're not more excited about Karl knowing he's one of those picture men," Gretchen said.

"Do you never stop and think, child?" Tante Klegg said from between clamped lips. "This is not the time or place to discuss Confederate sympathies."

Karl frowned. "Ain't no Confederate sympathies here. I took photos for my boss, that's all."

Gretchen gestured at him, glad he proved her point.

Tante Klegg ignored him. "He did not kill the president, but he could have killed others to avoid dying. Does he remember his family? Does he remember a girl?" Tante Klegg shook her head. "Headstrong, foolish, enthusiastic for no reason..."

Gretchen was ready to fight back, but the door opened. Black curtains covered every window of the statehouse so they could not peek inside. Above the door sat an inscription carved into wood: "God moves in a Mysterious Way."

Soldiers ushered them inside.

Mourners shuffled with tiny steps. Hoop skirts ballooned against each other. Men struggled not to trip over the voluminous fabrics. Gretchen craned her neck again, trying to see the president's casket. She could see the bier covered with piles and piles of lilacs. The casket crushed them; their sweet smell overpowered the room.

"Smart," Tante Klegg said.

Karl and Gretchen looked at her, aghast. What could be smart about viewing a dead body?

"The lilacs," she whispered, gesturing ahead of them. "They hide the smell of the president. They tried a new method, which they call 'embalming,' but it cannot be good yet. It is too new. He decays before our eyes."

Gretchen put her hand over her mouth. This was not what she had imagined. She wanted to see a serene president, not a decaying one. It would be better to not smell anything than to smell lilacs and know they hid putridity. She began to shrink back, no longer sure she wanted to pay her last respects.

"I didn't like him," a woman whispered to her companion nearby, "but he didn't deserve to go out like that."

"What a blessing that the rains broke as the president arrived at the statehouse," a woman replied. "It is sure to be ordained that this man has reached the heavenly gates."

Tears gathered in Gretchen's eyes. This was too much and not enough. Coming to Columbus and seeing the president in person was her life's adventure. And now that Gretchen was steps away from Mr. Lincoln's casket, she realized she did not want to do this at all. She wanted to go home, but she did not have a home. She wanted to hold her papa's hand, but she did not have a papa. She wanted to breathe, but the flowers were choking her. Or her corset was choking her. Gretchen's hair was pulled back and up high. She looked like a young woman rather than the girl she had been last week.

She could not breathe. She could not move.

Karl grabbed her hand and squeezed, hard. Gretchen made a strangled little noise that grabbed the attention of those around them.

Tante Klegg moved past them as if she had no idea who they were.

"Don't know if it helps, but you can lean on me," Karl whispered, not daring to look at her with his hand holding hers.

Gretchen nodded, grateful that he had distracted her panic.

Karl pulled her hand through his arm and patted it in place as he stepped forward. Gretchen hesitated, but feeling Karl's gentle pull allowed her feet to fall in step with his. She could see the end of the bier where "LINCOLN" was written in large white letters.

White bunting draped the sides of the bier. A large rug buffered the echoing of everyone's muddied boots across the rotunda's marble floor. They could see the foot of the casket. A large floral arrangement sat above Mr. Lincoln's stomach.

"We're almost through," Karl whispered.

Gretchen nodded, her mouth dry. They approached the head of the casket. She dreaded seeing Mr. Lincoln's face. They shuffled forward to find the casket was not open at all. A large white cross lay on top of the casket in stark relief.

Tante Klegg waited for them outside the doors on the other side of the rotunda. "Satisfied?" she asked.

Now that she was away from the cloying lilacs, Gretchen released Karl's arm. She squared her shoulders. "Not yet. We haven't found Papa."

Tante Klegg's eyes narrowed. "Gregory Miller is not your father, my Alric was. It is the errand of a fool errand to search for him."

"What's the harm?" Karl asked. "We take a look at the lists, he's either on them or he isn't, and we go back to Werner's farm."

Gretchen stomped away from them. "It isn't Werner's farm, and I'm going to find my father."

When Gretchen was out of earshot, Tante Klegg pushed Karl. "This is your opportunity."

Karl watched Gretchen's receding back and swaying skirts.

"Leave now or never leave her side. You must decide now," Tante Klegg said.

Karl shrugged and loped after Gretchen.

"Interesting," Tante Klegg mused.

TWENTY-EIGHT

Saturday, 29 April 1865 / Columbus, Ohio

They did not speak as they returned to the farm. Gretchen was glad. What could they say? That viewing the president's casket was anticlimactic? That seeing Gregory Miller on the killed-in-action list should have been a surprise? That they should have figured something in Columbus would trigger Karl's memory?

Gretchen had a terrible ache in her side that would not fade. The corset had dug into her when she dashed back to the wagon after seeing her father's name. She refused to let anyone see her tears. Without a word, Karl had helped her into the wagon before Tante Klegg could admonish her for making a scene.

Gretchen did not know why Karl persisted in pretending to care about her. They did not need to pretend their engagement was real in as large a city as Columbus. No one knew them there, and Alina had made it clear she did not want to see them before her wedding photo. Gretchen was Karl's nurse and a bad one at that, nothing more.

Gretchen alternated between clutching her pinched side and rubbing her forehead. She ignored the worried frown Karl kept throwing her way as Tante Klegg urged the horse home. She struggled to dampen the warm feeling of his hand holding hers in the statehouse rotunda. She hated that he had looked so gallant ripping up their copy of the killed-in-action list. She scowled.

It was annoying that Karl chose to return to the farm. If there were a time for him to escape Werner, Columbus had been it.

Karl was wasting his time worrying about Gretchen. He had his memories. He was not the president's murderer. No one had tried to arrest him in Columbus. Gretchen was sure he knew he could go as he pleased. Yet he sat beside her. Every time the wagon bounced, their arms brushed. Gretchen's cheeks felt hotter and hotter until she was sure she looked redder than a beet.

"Penny for your thoughts," Karl said, nudging her.

"Won't take less than a dollar," Gretchen said.

Tante Klegg snorted. "Nothing in your head is worth such extravagance."

"Can't you be nice for once?" Karl said.

"Why?" Tante Klegg said. Her shoulders hunched, and she slapped the reins. The horse lurched forward with an alarmed whinny. "Her problem is that the world is not what she imagined it to be, and she is not the person she thought she was. We must all learn that. Why treat her as though that is special?"

Karl leaned back. "What if it is special for some of us? What's wrong with that?"

Gretchen glared at him from beneath her bonnet brim. She did not need him to fight her battles. He winked at her. And blast it, she might have grinned.

Tante Klegg snorted again. "Yes, and you know because your memories returned. You know everything now. You have life experience and wisdom and friends and family again. Is there a special girl waiting for you? Have you remembered her?"

Karl rubbed the back of his neck. "Don't think I have a home or a girl to go back to."

Gretchen glanced at him, suspicious about his neutral tone.

"Pretty sure my parents gave me up to the soldiers so they could afford meat for my brother."

"What?" Gretchen said, horrified.

Tante Klegg's shoulders hunched higher.

"He, my brother, that is, got wounded. I never did find out the battle, wasn't even in the house long enough to hug my ma. But she had sent word I had to come home. It was worrisome since both my parents had disowned me when I refused to fight. But family is family, ain't that right, Ms. Klegg? And if they called me home it had to be for good reason, I thought." His voice trailed, and he stared at the trees in the distance.

Gretchen bit the inside of her cheek to stop herself from demanding to know more. If he did not tell her the rest, she was going to push him out of the wagon and make him walk the rest of the way home.

"Anyway," Karl sighed, rousing, "all I remember is the blue coats were in the door before I took my hat off. They said I was a spy. I wasn't, but that didn't stop no one."

"So you won't be leaving, then," Gretchen said.

He grinned. "Reckon not. Unless they want to sell me to some other army."

"Sell you?" Gretchen said, recoiling. "Like a slave?"

"You can be this flippant about never returning to your home?" Tante Klegg said.

"Not all departures are bad," Karl said. "I hated being in that prison, but at least I knew where I stood with my family."

Tante Klegg's nostrils flared. "And what will you do now? Will you return to Southern slaveholding ways?"

Karl shuddered. "We didn't own slaves; too poor. Anyway, been on the receiving end of having no control over my life for too long. Don't know why I'd want control over someone's life like that."

"Because it gives you power," Tante Klegg said.

Karl shook his head. "Not the type any sane person wants. Sooner or later, all slaves, all prisoners, revolt. All beings can sense they're meant for something more than working and dying."

Gretchen listened, unsure what to make of this. She knew all Confederates owned slaves because the papers said so. She knew all Confederates wanted to destroy the Union, and Booth came close to succeeding.

Yet, here sat Karl, gaining pieces of his memory every minute, saying he was never a slave owner. And he was never a soldier, but a war photographer. And he was not sent to prison for a war crime, but because his heartless family gave him up for the favorite sibling.

Gretchen could relate to that. "I can't believe Pa's dead," she whispered. "Only, he was never my pa."

Karl held open his hand in the small space between his leg and Gretchen's skirts out of sight from Tante Klegg. Gretchen laid her hand in his after a small hesitation.

"I never had a father, I guess," Gretchen said.

Tante Klegg's posture hunched further, her expression turned thunderous.

"Oh, I don't know," Karl said. "He left you the revolver and taught you how to shoot and to protect the farm. Sounds like he took an interest. More than mine, anyhow. My pa always thought me weak and sickly, so he poured attention at my brother." He frowned, concentrating. "Must have crushed Pa when... when... my brother returned without his legs."

Gretchen shivered. Bad enough to lose an arm, but to lose a leg, or both? A farmer needed his legs. Might as well have stayed on the battlefield to die. "What is his name?"

Karl turned. "What do you mean?"

"You keep calling him 'your brother.' He had a name, you have a name." Gretchen shrugged, tilting her head up to peer at him from under her bonnet. "What is his name?"

"Well, I'm... Elias..." Karl said. His expression slipped into a panic as he began to stutter. "H-h-h-his... his n-n-n—n-n-n..." He clapped his hand over his mouth.

"I'm sorry. You don't have to answer," Gretchen said, eyes wide.

Karl shook his head. He closed his eyes and inhaled. "His name was A-a-a-ambrose." His voice trailed off as Tante Klegg pulled into the farmyard.

"Ambrose and Elias. Those are fine names," Gretchen said.

Karl's smile was wan. "Looks like Alina and Werner are back," he said. The pastor's buggy was waiting outside the house. He hopped from the wagon and helped Tante Klegg down. She set to removing the horse tack, otherwise ignoring Karl.

Gretchen moved to hop from the wagon like Karl, but stopped short when the corset bit her side.

Karl held out his hands.

Rolling her eyes, Gretchen allowed him to take her waist and lift her off the wagon. She pulled away as soon as her toes touched the ground, but not before realizing how easy it would be to tip her chin up and kiss his cheek.

"Don't get any stupid ideas," she said, warning herself as much as Karl. "I'm dressed like a lady, but I can still shoot an apple off your head."

"Stupid's my middle name," Karl said, shoving his hands in his pockets as he followed Gretchen.

Gretchen shook her head. "How you can joke at a time like this..."

"Time like what? I ain't killed anyone. Even in the war I wasn't a soldier. I'm not your enemy. Never was. And since you nursed me back to health, gave me the opportunity to know myself, don't see how I ever will be."

"Oh, I don't know," Gretchen said. "Everyone else has taken their turn."

TWENTY-NINE

Saturday, 29 April 1865 / Columbus, Ohio

Werner sat at the table, allowing Alina to feed him dinner as if he were a child. He held the revolver in his lap and watched them suspiciously. Before the war, Gretchen would have taunted him for being paranoid. Before the war, Werner would not have pointed a weapon at her. Before the war, he had both of his hands. Before the war, they had a father.

Werner wore a uniform given by one of the families in town who had lost their son. Gretchen saw dark circles under Alina and Adelaide's eyes. They must have spent the night polishing the brass buttons and brushing the navy wool.

Gretchen stared at her cousin. She saw the cocky boy who had left and the disfigured man who had returned without a kind word for anyone.

Tante Klegg lifted the still steaming coffee pot from the table. She handed it to Gretchen, who poured three deep saucers for herself, Tante Klegg, and Karl. It was a family tradition to pour their coffee into saucers so the liquid cooled by the time they brought it to their lips. Gretchen wondered if this would be her last time enjoying coffee with her family.

"Why, Gretchen," Alina exclaimed. She dropped her fork. "You look so...adult!"

"Well, I guess I should, since I am one," Gretchen said. She lifted her saucer and blew across it.

Karl followed her lead before gulping the coffee down. They had not eaten since morning, and it was past sunset. He eyed the loaf of bread at the table, but did not move when Werner shifted the aim of the revolver in his direction.

"That is an odd thing to say," Alina said, looking around the room. "What does she mean?"

"Not only am I not Werner's sister," Gretchen said. She crossed her arms over her stomach. "I'm older than him, and Tante—er, Mama Klegg—decided I should dress my true age."

Alina stared at Gretchen, dumbstruck.

"Are you planning on using that?" Gretchen said, gesturing at the revolver in Werner's hand.

"Maybe," Werner said, not taking his eyes from Karl. "I don't like the look of this one."

Gretchen held her saucer with both hands and sipped. "Has anyone told you what a terrible host you are?"

Tante Klegg glared at Gretchen. "How was your portrait session? Did you have time to see the president?" she asked Alina.

Alina clapped her hands together. "It was magical! We put it on our mantle. Does it look nice?" She gestured at the fireplace opposite the stove.

"*Your* mantle?" Gretchen said. "How dare you—"

"How do you mean, magical?" Tante Klegg said, interrupting Gretchen. "I have never been. I would like to know everything." She walked over to the mantle and studied the photo.

Karl followed. They had taken one photo and framed it in gold gilt. They had not paid for any sort of coloring. It was a tintype on reflective metal, the cheapest option. Werner sat on a plush, high-backed chair. Alina stood beside him, resting her hand on his shoulder and hiding his missing arm behind her skirts. He looked stern, she looked shy. It was a perfect composition.

"This is fine work," Karl said.

"No one asked you," Werner said.

Gretchen plopped into the remaining open chair at the table. Adelaide glowered at her.

Alina described how the photographer put Werner in the chair out of respect for a war veteran. How she stood beside him, in such a way so her skirts would mask his...delicacy.

"Don't be stupid," Werner said. "No amount of skirts is going to hide my lost arm."

"Werner, my child, your wife says these things to be kind to you," Adelaide said.

"Who asked her to be kind to me?" Werner said. "I don't need kindness, I need my arm."

"I'm your wife," Alina whispered. She stared into her lap. "Are you not happy that we married?"

Werner closed his eyes. "Of course I—look, I wrote that when I was a child, before all this happened. It's not that I don't want to be your husband, but I never thought it would be like this."

Gretchen frowned. "How old was that letter, Alina?"

Alina blanched.

Gretchen stood and placed her palms on the table as she leaned closer. "How old was that letter?"

Alina cleared her throat. "Three years?"

Tante Klegg choked on her coffee. Adelaide's saucer crashed to the floor. It took every ounce of willpower for Gretchen to resist throwing herself across the table at Alina's jaw. Karl grabbed her elbow, dragging her from the table.

"And how much of that letter was real?" Gretchen demanded. "Did Werner write that he wanted a double wedding or not?"

Werner glared at Alina, but she would not look up from her lap. "Linnie," he said, his tone patronizing. "Did you falsify my letter?"

Alina shook her head. "I added to it."

Werner's mouth gaped open.

"My cousin's wife is a gifted artist, isn't she, *Tante Miller?*" Gretchen cast a sarcastic look at Adelaide. "She can mimic handwriting, it seems, so no one can tell the difference. Such a trustworthy girl to bring into this saint-like family of ours." Gretchen laughed. "Never fear, Alina. You belong."

"You're one to talk," Alina said. "Hiding a Confederate in this house! Letting me think you were going to marry him!"

"Who said anything about him being a Confederate?" Gretchen said.

"I am not the fool you take me for," Alina screamed. "Do you think I cannot hear his accent?"

"Who said anything about Gretchen marrying anyone?" Werner said.

"You did, in your stupid letter," Gretchen breathed. Her corset was fighting her again. "You wanted to have a silly double wedding."

"I wrote no such thing," Werner said.

THIRTY

Saturday, 29 April 1865 / Columbus, Ohio

"I never meant to marry Karl," Gretchen said. She had to say this. She had to protect Karl. She knew that look on Werner's face. Someone had to pay for making him feel this way and Karl was just too convenient. "I wanted to help him. I had hoped some southerner would do the same for my brother."

Gretchen wiped her hand down her face. "But I guess it was all for nothing. Werner isn't my brother. Look at him—he doesn't want my help or anyone else's; he's all-fired mad about his arm. And Karl, here! He went along with Alina's dumb idea to make him my *verlobter*."

"Explains why she's so mad," Karl said. "Caught in her own lies. Can't feel too good."

Werner stared at Alina as if he did not know her. Alina stared back, defiant.

"I was the one who said Karl should be your *verlobter*," Tante Klegg corrected. "Alina's letter was... convenient to hide Karl's identity."

"My name's Elias, not Karl," he said.

Gretchen snorted. "No one here is who they said they were."

Karl crossed his arms over his chest, frowning. "I'm the only one in this room who hasn't lied to you. Don't take your anger out on me."

"All right then," Gretchen said, "*Elias.*"

"Must you have to ruin this day?" Adelaide said. "This day on which we celebrate my son's wedding?"

"You thought today was going to be about Werner, on the day when the president's body came to town?" Gretchen countered, glaring at her. "You thought you could celebrate on a day of statewide mourning? Tante Klegg was right. I'm *nothing* like you. And I'm glad."

Adelaide turned away.

"This never would have happened if you'd gotten married," Alina said. "You'd be out of this house and out of our hair. Damn your little Confederate for ruining everything!"

"Hey now," Karl, that is, Elias, said. He made sure to look everyone in the eye before continuing. "Can we get one thing clear here? Y'all didn't need my help ruining things. You'd have gotten there one way or another. Now, I marched with the Confederate army to help take photos of the war, but they captured me while on leave."

Werner stared at Elias, his entire body trembling. His eyes about popped out of their sockets, he was so mad that Elias dared speak to him.

"But I ain't a Confederate because I can't be," Elias continued. He turned to Gretchen now, seeking her full attention. "To get released from Camp Chase, I had to take an oath of allegiance to the Union. Like it or not, I may have been on the wrong side once, but I'm one of you now so stop your fussing."

There was a long, glorious moment of stunned silence.

Gretchen burst into laughter. Everyone stared at her as if she had lost her mind.

"All this time," she wheezed, "we thought... *I* thought we had Mr. Lincoln's murderer in our house. We thought we had a Confederate in our house. Two weeks of running around afraid the Union army would descend on our farm. And none of it was true!"

Adelaide straightened her shoulders. "You can say whatever you want in your pretty little accent to my niece," she said to Elias. "We are not stupid. To take those photographs, you had to pledge allegiance to someone. It was not Mr. Lincoln, and it was not the stars and stripes."

Elias's mouth dropped open. "Are you serious? I remember who I am. Why don't you believe me? I'm a United States citizen now!"

Adelaide's chin lifted. She lifted the fork from the table and stirred Werner's potatoes to warm them a little. Werner smirked.

"My name's Elias Jones. I was a photographer's assistant and colorist, and yes, I worked for a man loyal to the Confederacy. But what was the Confederacy to me? Second son of a poor farmer who wasn't going to benefit anyway." Elias scratched the bandage covering his temple. "Can't go back home. They'll kill me." He turned to Gretchen. "What do you think they were trying to do when they handed me off to those soldiers?"

"But you still have all your limbs, don't you?" Werner said. He wiggled the stump that was his right arm.

His mother whimpered and looked away. Alina's hand with the fork wavered, then kept stirring.

"I want to know why," Gretchen said to Alina between gasps. "Why add to Werner's letter?"

"Shut up, Gretchen," Werner said, aiming the revolver at Elias.

Gretchen ground her teeth together when Elias's hand made her stay put. Not that she fancied facing the mean end of a revolver, but she hated seeing it dance in Elias's face like that.

"You want to know why?" Alina said. "Because you are willful."
Tante Klegg inhaled.

"Mama warned me. She said I could not marry into a family with a girl who could not be corrected. It would bring our family down. I have younger sisters. There aren't many men anymore, Gretchen! I can't do that to my sisters. And I love Werner so much! More than you ever did. I had to stop you, make you settle down and marry."

Gretchen stared at Alina, seeing her for the first time. Her simpering smile hid hard, calculating eyes that studied Gretchen's every move.

"I guess I should give you more credit," Gretchen said. "I never thought the pastor's daughter could be so manipulative."

"Get out," Werner whispered. He raised his voice. "Get out of my house." He aimed at Elias. "Get out of my sight!"

Gretchen knew there were a great many stupid ideas that she had had in her short life. Still, she figured stepping in front of her cousin's revolver to protect a Confederate had to be the most stupid. Not that it stopped her. She held her arms out and planted her feet wider than hips-width apart.

"Don't you dare shoot my prisoner," Gretchen said.

THIRTY-ONE

Saturday, 29 April 1865 / Columbus, Ohio

Elias cleared his throat to grab Gretchen's attention. He tilted his head, glaring at her. This was not the time to fly off the handle. She did not have a revolver to make Werner see reason.

"You're nothing but a dirty Copperhead," Werner said. "You're not my sister, and I don't want you as my cousin. I want you out of my house. You will not spend another night under the same roof as my wife."

Gretchen fell back. Her face stung as if he had slapped her with all his might. She was not a Copperhead. She was against the Confederacy and all it stood for. She hated the Confederates for breaking up the Union. She hated the Confederates for breaking up her family. She hated the Confederates for breaking her cousin.

Gretchen looked at Elias, who nodded at her. Tante Klegg grunted and stepped back. Gretchen did not think too hard about it. She launched herself at Werner. Elias was close behind. The screams of his wife and mother almost drowned out the explosion of the revolver firing. The lead ball went through the slatted ceiling as Werner landed on the puncheon floor with a hard thud.

Werner grunted when Gretchen shifted her weight so most of it was on him. This was difficult because her hoop skirt had popped up when she threw herself to the ground. She managed to keep Werner still so Elias could wrestle the revolver from him.

"Will you shut up?" Gretchen shouted at Adelaide and Alina.

Alina complied, whimpering and wringing her hands together. Adelaide stopped screaming, but the words she said instead would have made a hardened soldier blush.

Tante Klegg considered the dramatic scene. She held Werner's bedroom door open and waved inside.

"You help them?" Adelaide said.

"Your son did not abide by his promise," Tante Klegg replied. "He said we had until Monday. Yet he waves a weapon in our face on Saturday when we should all be reflecting on the state of our nation."

"Is this the son you've pined for, Mama Miller?" Gretchen said, sitting on a wriggling Werner. "A son who left the war because he grew tired of it? A son who threatens unarmed women because of a temper tantrum?"

Adelaide glared at her.

Gretchen punched Werner hard in his side. He groaned and tried to curl into a fetal position, but could not because Gretchen still sat on him. Elias pointed the revolver at his head.

"How do you think life will be like with this person?" Gretchen asked Adelaide. "Do you think his return is worth all those years of being cruel to me?"

"He is my son," she said. "You cannot understand."

Tante Klegg reached into the bedroom to retrieve the rope that once held the door shut at night. With Elias maintaining a lock on Werner, Tante Klegg helped Gretchen tie Werner's hand to his ankles.

"You would hogtie your own cousin?" Alina whimpered.

"Oh, stop it, Alina," Gretchen said. "How can you be so naïve to marry a man without waiting to see how the war changed him?"

Alina scowled. "You think you are so smart," she said. "I am a wife now. I am important to society. You are a nuisance." She lifted her skirts and joined Adelaide by Werner's bedroom door.

Elias tucked the revolver in the back of his pants to help Gretchen and Tante Klegg haul Werner off the floor. It was not difficult to do with Werner's malnourished weight. Gretchen and Tante Klegg shouldered Werner. Elias trained the revolver on Alina and Adelaide.

"If you please," Elias said in his nicest voice, gesturing in the direction of Werner's bedroom with a little bow.

Alina and Adelaide sat on Werner's bed and watched Gretchen and Tante Klegg dump Werner on the floor in front of them. They said nothing as Gretchen and Tante Klegg backed out of the room, Elias guarding them the entire way.

Tante Klegg shut the door. They heard a loud shuffling noise followed by a startling thump against the door.

"He's trying to kick his way through," Gretchen said.

The door began to shudder. Werner was making progress, and he screamed his fury. Gretchen could only imagine what it was like on the other side—Alina and Adelaide cowering on the bed, her hogtied cousin kicking his way to insanity.

The hinges began to rattle. Elias leapt to hold the door in place. Tante Klegg ran from the room.

"Now Gretchen," Elias grunted, "I know I've only known you a little while. But it's been a busy two weeks. And I know that you think this is your home, but it's becoming mighty clear that it's not."

Gretchen rolled her eyes. She braced the door to help him. "Now what makes you think that?"

Elias cleared his throat and raised his voice over Werner's shouts and kicks. "I don't know what you think, but we get along all right."

Gretchen's eyes narrowed.

"Uh... it wouldn't be so bad to do as your aunt—your ma—" Elias stumbled to correct himself under Gretchen's suspicious glare. "Anyway, maybe you'd consider marrying me."

"What?" Werner shrieked through the door.

"Maybe we'd drive each other nuts. Maybe we'd be good companions. Don't know for sure either way," Elias rushed.

Tante Klegg walked between them with a hammer and pounded at a hinge, mangling it. She acted as if Elias and Gretchen were not staring each other down.

"Could we talk about this some other time?" Gretchen said through gritted teeth.

Tante Klegg bent, hammering and mangling another hinge.

"All you got is your ma and me. And I ain't got nobody but you two. So it's up to you. Not going to make you make up your mind now—"

"Generous of you," Gretchen said.

"But I wanted to put it out there that I'm not opposed to marrying if you're not."

Gretchen closed her eyes and waited for Tante Klegg to finish the third hinge. When the room fell quiet, she said, "You think this is the best time to be talking like this? We locked my family—*we kidnapped my family*—in a bedroom and you decide now's the time to propose?"

Tante Klegg snickered, took one look at Gretchen, and walked back outside to the barn. "I will get the wagon ready," she called over her shoulder.

Elias shrugged. "Didn't seem any other time to do it."

Gretchen crossed her arms over her chest.

"We do it now or we're spending our days with your ma—yes, your ma, Gretchen. She'll be chaperoning us as if we're courting when we're on the run and that... seems odd. To me."

Gretchen's nostrils flared, and her eyes flashed.

"You have to admit it don't ever seem to be a good time for anything, so I figured I might as well just ask."

"Unbelievable," was her reply. Gretchen stomped up the stairs to her attic bedroom with Elias staring after her.

Werner began kicking against the door again with more fervor. Elias watched the door shake.

Gretchen stumbled down the stairs, having thrown everything she owned in a carpetbag. "Come on," she said. "You got one thing right. We're not staying here anymore."

THIRTY-TWO

Saturday, 29 April 1865 / Columbus, Ohio

Gretchen threw supplies at Elias, and he threw them into the wagon amidst Werner's screams. Gretchen avoided looking at him, so Elias had to duck under a flying bag of flour and dive to catch a packet of bacon. He stumbled under the force of Gretchen's carpetbag shoved into his arms. "Hey now."

She ran to the barn and back, dodging Tante Klegg guiding the horse as she carried Elias's haversack. She tossed it atop the carpetbag, which he had placed in the wagon. "Your things."

Elias pulled the drawstring open with shaking hands. So much had happened since last opening the haversack. He had assumed she had burned it with his ratty prison clothes.

It was hard to believe he had left Camp Chase only a couple of weeks ago. Fresh water filled the canteen; Gretchen must have filled it. The jar of pickled onions remained unopened. He rubbed the haversack's canvas fabric between his fingers and felt a sharp edge. He turned it inside out to find a small metal daguerreotype of a man, woman, and two boys. He ran his thumb over the face most like his.

He would never know who had saved him from the prison. He would never know why that person had decided to be his godsend. Elias looked up from the knapsack to find Gretchen watching him.

"You know," Elias mused, "before the war, people said, 'The United States are.'"

Gretchen crossed her arms.

Tante Klegg harnessed the horse to the wagon. She clucked, shaking her head at the shaking house. "The time for speaking is over. We must leave now." She climbed onto the wagon and tied her bonnet strings.

Elias handed Gretchen the small metal square. "That's what they were, you know. Plural. Colonies banding together because they hated the British empire."

Gretchen held the daguerreotype with both hands, staring at it. "We joined together to fight for our freedom."

Tante Klegg motioned that Gretchen should climb aboard the wagon. Gretchen ignored her, waiting to hear what Elias had to say.

"Don't know a whole lot about Mr. Lincoln," Elias said, making Gretchen stiffen. "But I can tell he was a good man by the things the people at the funeral said about him. He tried his best. He didn't deserve to die that way."

Gretchen shook her head. Tears gathered in her eyes and threatened to spill. "Neither did my papa."

Elias scratched the fabric wrapped around his forehead and began to unwind it. "No one deserved it. They fought because they believed in a greater nation. A united nation." Elias ran his fingers through his hair. "You don't deserve to be homeless because you fought for me."

Gretchen handed the metal photo back to Elias and waved at the house. Werner's screams grew hoarse and curse-laden. "I would have ended up homeless anyway."

Elias bunched the bandage in his hands. "Look, Gretchen, I meant what I said in there. You're a good person, and you've been good to me. And you're smart. And funny. You take care of your own, and not your own."

Her cheeks started to color, and she kicked a rock.

"Could you speak faster?" Tante Klegg said. "We do not know how long that door will hold Werner."

"Let him speak his piece!" Gretchen said.

Tante Klegg spun in her seat, grumbling.

Elias found himself blushing. "Don't have much else to say. I'm asking if you want to have the pastor marry us, but if you say no, I won't bother you again."

Gretchen climbed onto the wagon and reached down for his hand to help him up beside her. "Nothing would annoy Alina more than her pa marrying us."

The kitchen door slammed open. Bullets sprayed from the house.

Gretchen screamed, ducking behind the side of the wagon. Tante Klegg slapped the reins, making the horse jump into a healthy trot.

Elias's mouth dropped open.

"Elias!" Gretchen shouted, arm outstretched as the wagon bounced away.

Elias had no idea if he was a good runner. A bullet whizzed past his ear. He decided any form of running was better than standing still. He sprinted, reaching for Gretchen. She grasped his hand and yanked when he jumped. Elias crashed into Gretchen, and they both fell to the wagon bed.

Gretchen froze underneath him. He rolled away, clutching the wagon walls to keep from getting too close.

"You must say yes to him now," Tante Klegg called over her shoulder.

Gretchen made a face at her. She watched Werner chase them for a couple of yards before falling from exhaustion. Alina dropped to the ground with him, cradling his head in her lap as he sobbed.

"Tell me about this united nation," Gretchen said to Elias. She stared as the only home she had known disappeared from vie.

Elias cleared his throat. "We've had a reckoning with ourselves, and I guess it was due. You don't think we'll start to hear 'the United States is'? Single? One nation?"

Gretchen pressed her lips together as she pondered this. She liked the sound of a single nation. She was glad to hear the hope in Elias's voice, because her hope was lacking these days. Her own cousin had tried to kill her, even though she had prayed for him to return home for years. Her papa was gone. The woman she called her mama had disowned her.

"One nation. Forged with the blood of brothers and fathers and uncles," Gretchen whispered.

"And sisters and wives and aunts," Elias said.

The wagon bounced down the road. The horse slowed to a walk once Tante Klegg realized Werner had stopped chasing them.

Gretchen crawled across the wagon to sit beside Elias. She took his hand and held it in her lap as she rested her head against his shoulder. "Mr. Lincoln wanted the country to come back together."

Elias held his breath.

"And I swore I'd do my part." Gretchen smirked at Elias. "But don't worry. I'm not saying yes because I'm a patriot."

Elias's eyebrows shot up. "Then why are you?"

"Because you..." Gretchen laughed, a little breathless. "You saw me."

Elias nodded. "I see you."

The sun shone in high contrast from the clouds that gathered behind them. Gretchen, holding Elias's hand, studied Tante Klegg's back. Tante Klegg, her mother who never was and yet always had been. That was the sort of love worth holding onto, Gretchen realized. Noble, honest, and sacrificing. It was that sort of dedication that would bring the nation back together.

Gretchen smiled at Elias. "The United States *is* exactly where I'll find my home." She kissed his cheek and paid no mind to Tante Klegg's grunt.

German Phrases

- *Mütter* (n). mother

- *Vater* (n). father

- *Tante* (n). aunt

- *Verlobter* (n). betrothed, male

- *Liebchen* (n). term of endearment

- *Meine kleine schweister* — "My little sister"

- *Meine kleine trottel* — "My little idiot"

- *Kleines mädchen* — "Little girl"

- *Fräulein* — "Miss"

- *Größe Deutsch* — "Greater Germany"

Reading Guide

1. Why do you think this book was named *The Last April*?
2. Do the location and environment of the book color the telling of the story or are they merely a backdrop?
3. How do the character perspectives color the story of life in Ohio after the president's assassination?
4. What are some of the parallels between Lincoln's assassination, Pearl Harbor, and 9/11 in American history?
5. Do you believe Gretchen's motivations in bringing Karl/Elias into her home?
6. Would you open your home to someone you consider an enemy?
7. Did reading this book help you to understand a person better, or even yourself?

Author's Note

The Last April is a novel set in 1865 Central Ohio. At its heart, this is a story of "what is happening to the nation?" versus "what is happening to me?" that most individuals face at some point in their lives.

Abraham Lincoln's assassination was the 1865 version of the September 11, 2011 tragedy. The more I learned about the nation's reaction and panic in the days following Abraham Lincoln's death, the more I wondered. Imagine 9/11 without social media, radio, or television. Where would you get your news? How would you know your sources were credible?

Can you believe it took almost a week for the Midwest to catch up to and make sense of the news coming from the D.C. area? The newspapers are telling. One city claimed all three politicians died (false). Another city claimed two lived (true).

Here are some things I learned while writing this historical story.

Lincoln's Assassination

Assassination of President Lincoln by Currier & Ives Lithography Co.

Abraham Lincoln died from the first successful assassination attempt in the nation's history. There were other assassination attempts on other presidents, though. An unsuccessful attempt occurred thirty years prior against Andrew Jackson. Mr. Lincoln often had nightmares about dying. He even had one vivid dream where he walked into a White House parlor to find an open casket. Upon asking who had the misfortune to die, someone said, "The president."

John Wilkes Booth shot Mr. Lincoln on Good Friday, April 14, 1865. John Wilkes Booth was a famous actor (more below) and Confederate sympathizer. Lincoln attended the play *Our American*

Cousin with his wife. It was their first "date" since winning the war. Lincoln hoped to mend his hurting marriage with his wife after the hardship of war and losing a child.

Instead, during a moment when the audience was loud, Booth shot Lincoln in the back of the head in his private box. Mrs. Mary Todd Lincoln began screaming. Booth jumped to the stage, shouting, "Sic semper tyrannis." This translates to "Thus always to tyrants."

John Wilkes Booth

It rocked the nation when Booth shot Lincoln, not only because it happened, but because of who did it. A short, slight man, Booth was the sort of man other men wanted to be and the ladies wanted to court.

Imagine Justin Timberlake or Zac Efron plotting to kill the president. John Wilkes Booth was one of the most popular actors of the time. Girls—Yankee and Rebel—kept photos of him under their pillows.

The night of Lincoln's death, there were two other planned attacks. Lewis Powell was to kill Secretary of State William Seward. George Atzerodt was to kill Vice President Andrew Johnson. Powell did break into Seward's house and stabbed him and his son. Atzerodt got drunk and never left the bar.

Booth escaped Maryland but struggled to make it back to the Confederate states. Union soldiers set fire to the barn he hid in, and shot him so he lost control of his arms and legs. He died without apologizing. His diary shows he expected everyone to applaud his efforts. His entries show he was angry the newspapers did not treat him as a hero.

Civil War Photography

The Civil War encouraged photography to blossom in the United States. The Civil War was the most documented war in the nineteenth century, and the fifth in all history (as of 2017). It was the first war to use photos as war propaganda. It was also the first to use photos to help loved ones feel close to those at the battlefront.

Thanks to these photographs, we can see the young age of so many soldiers, Union and Confederate. We know how bodies were strewn across the battlefield. We know how generals conferred with their staff between battles. To learn more, research Union photographers Matthew Brady, Alexander Gardner, and Timothy O'Sullivan.

We don't know a lot about the Confederate photographers. Many burned their originals when the war ended, out of despair, anger, and fear. We know many families burned photographs of their departed loved ones. Think of it as a sort of hysteria at having lost their family *and* the war. To learn more, research Confederate photographers George S. Cook, James Osborn, and Lieutenant Robert M. Smith. Lieutenant Smith was a Confederate imprisoned on Johnson's Island in Ohio from Lake Erie. He made a wet plate camera from trash! You can read more about him and Yankee prison life in David S. Bush's *I Fear I Shall Never Leave This Island*.

Germans in Ohio and the Civil War

About ten percent of the 2.2 million Union soldiers were of German-descent. Many of the German emigrants at the time had fled persecution of the educated elite. The United States received Germanic philosophers and idealists. Others fled to escape the brutal infighting from their own 1856 civil war.

Either way, they made a large contribution to American society.

Ohio and the Civil War

Lincoln is often quoted as saying, "Ohio won the war." Many attribute this comment to the 320,000 Ohio men who volunteered for battle. This was the third highest number after New York and Pennsylvania. Almost 35,500 died in the line of duty, or of wounds, disease, drowning, murder, and other causes unstated.

Without the help of Ohio's men, it's hard to say what would have happened with the Civil War. All we can say is that those huge numbers bolstered the Union Army to counter the Confederate's.

To learn more,

- Visit the Ohio History Connection

- Refer to my list of resources at the end of this book

- Visit Grove City's Century Village

Once a year, Grove City's Century Village hosts a Civil War reenactment, where you can visit blacksmiths, a goods store, regiment training, and authentic buildings.

In fact, stories from Grove City elders inspired a couple of the smaller details in this novel.

Morgan's Raid

There were two Confederate prisons in Ohio: Camp Chase in Columbus and Johnson's Island in Sandusky. There were no battles in Ohio, unless you count Morgan's infamous raid in 1863.

Many do not know of the raid because it happened on the same dates as the battles of Vicksburg and Gettysburg. Confederate newspapers called the forty-six day trek the "Great Raid of 1863." This is because the cavalry hit places in Tennessee, Kentucky, Indiana, and Ohio. Union newspapers referred to it as the "Calico Raid." This is because the raiders stole from small stores and civilians.

Brigadier General John Hunt Morgan's Confederate cavalry struck fear into the civilian population. They distracted tens of hundreds of Union troops from their duties. They threatened the Ohio River trade and commerce. Morgan surrendered in Ohio and was imprisoned in the Columbus penitentiary. In a daring escape, Morgan and three of his officers dug a tunnel through their prison cell air shafts. They boarded a train and were in Cincinnati by the next morning.

Morgan's raid was ineffectual. It caused the Confederates to lose a cavalry unit and rallied Union forces. It also influenced prisoner treatment in Ohio for the remaining two years of the war.

Camp Chase

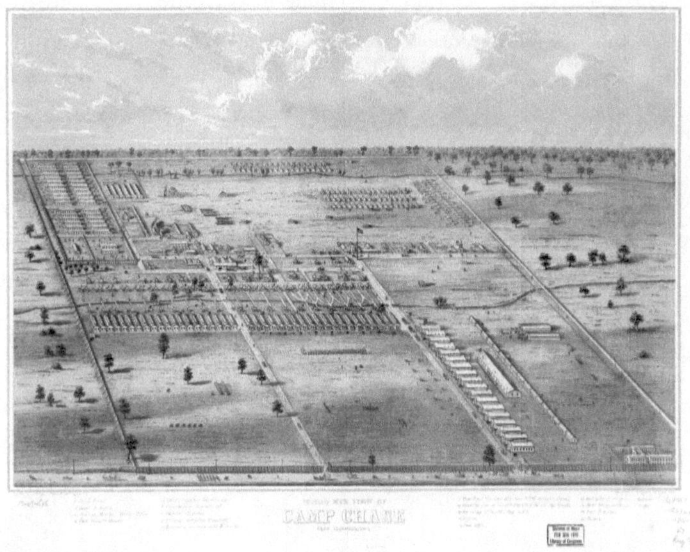

Camp Chase was never meant to be a prison. It was a recruitment, training, and mustering out barracks. Four future presidents passed through Camp Chase as Union soldiers and guards. Can you name them?[1]

Camp Chase also housed Confederate and political prisoners of war from 1862 – 1865. As a prison, the populace overcrowded the shanty buildings. There were never enough guards to watch the prisoners. As such, guards often used martial law to maintain order. Guards shot a prisoner because he started a fire in the middle of the night one winter. They shot another in the leg for stepping over a line after mishearing instructions.

The government decommissioned Camp Chase almost immediately after the war. By July 1865, the government exchanged, released, or moved all prisoners. By May 1866, only a single guard

---

1. Andrew Johnson, Rutherford B. Hayes, James Garfield, and William McKinley.

protected the entire campgrounds. By 1867, lumber from the camp was used to build a wall around the cemetery. All that's left of the camp today is the cemetery.

The Camp Chase cemetery is the largest Confederate cemetery outside of the Confederacy. It is in Columbus, Ohio in the Hilltop neighborhood. You may tour the cemetery and visit the yearly June remembrance ceremony for all who died in Camp Chase.

This remembrance ceremony began with the 1895 work of William H. Knauss, a former Union soldier, who honored those who died in the camp with an inscribed boulder. It remains there today and reads, "2260 Confederate soldiers of the war 1861-1865 buried in this enclosure." He also commissioned a statue with its single, telling inscription, "Americans."

Acknowledgments

Thank you for joining me on this adventure. Your time and imagination are precious.

Navigating microfilm is dizzying and gives me headaches. Thank you, Ohio History Connection and Library of Congress for digitizing *The Ohio Daily Statesman*!

The writer's group at Wild Goose Creative kept me accountable to my passion. I am glad my parents empowered my reading habits as a child, which often meant I did not do the dishes until bedtime (but I did do them!) Thank you especially to my editor, Cindy Sherwood, for spending hours to correct my inconsistencies, and to Allison Lodico and John Wiley for providing invaluable reader feedback. And to Allison's 2016-2017 5th Grade class for helping choose the title of this book!

Thank you to my doggies for cuddles when inspiration was lacking. Thank you to my funny husband who related to me by playing his childhood favorite computer game, W.R. Hutsell's *VGA Civil War Strategy*. Thank you, hun, for letting me stay up late on work nights so I could write "one more word."

References

(ALL SOURCES ARE INTENDED FOR ADULT READERS)

Archive.org. 'Selected Records of the War Department Relating to Confederate Prisoners of War, 1861-1865 [Microform]'. N. p., 2014. Web. 26 Jun. 2014.

Barbiere, Joseph. *Scraps from the prison table: at Camp Chase and Johnson's Island*. W.W.H Davis, 1868.

Barrett, Richard. *Images of America: Columbus 1860-1910*. Chicago, IL: Arcadio Publishing, 2005.

Clay, Paul; Ongaro, Patti; and Neff, Lois. *The Men and Women of Camp Chase*. The Hilltop Historical Society.

Dodds, Gilbert F. *Early Agriculture in Franklin County*. 1st ed. Columbus, Ohio: Franklin County Historical Society, 1954. Print.

Griswold, Manfred M. 'Ohio Civil War 150 | Collections & Exhibits | Prison Interior, Camp Chase, Ca. 1861-1865'. Ohiocivilwar150.org. N. p., 2013. Web. 6 May. 2013.

Henry, John King. *Three Hundred Days In A Yankee Prison: Reminiscenses Of War Life, Captivity, Imprisonment At Camp Chase, Ohio, Vol 18*. 1st ed. Atlanta: J.P. Daves, 1904. Print.

Hammock, Paul. "Reconstructing the South." *Echoes in Time Theatre, Ohio History Connection*. 27 June 2015. 1 PM EST.

References

Immigration and Ethnic Heritage in Ohio to 1903. 1st ed. Ohio Memory, 2012. Web. 11 Jul. 2013.

Ivy Morris, Jack Jr. 'Camp Chase, Columbus OH, 1861 – 1865: A Study of the Union's Treatment of Confederate Prisoners of War.' PhD. The University of Alabama, 1990. Print.

Jacksontwp.org. *'History | Jackson Township'.* Web. 4 Jun. 2014.

Jones, Robert Leslie. *Ohio Agriculture During the Civil War.* 1st ed. [Columbus]: Ohio State University Press for the Ohio Historical Society, 1962. Print.

Kelbaugh, Ross J. *Introduction to Civil War Photography.* 1st ed. Gettysburg, PA: Thomas Publications, 1991. Print.

Knauss, William H. *The Story of Camp Chase: A History of the Prison and its Cemetery Together with Other Cemeteries where Confederate Prisoners Are Buried.* 1st ed. Nashville, Tenn., Dallas, Tex.: Pub. House of the Methodist Episcopal Church, South, Smith & Lamar, agents, 1906. Print.

Lee, Alfred E. *History of The City of Columbus, Capital Of Ohio.* 1st ed. New York: Munsell & Co., 1892. Print.

Lentz, Edward R. *Columbus: The Story of a City (OH).* 1st ed. Charleston, SC: Arcadia Pub., 2003. Print.

Lentz, Edward R. *Historic Columbus: A Bicentennial History.* 1st ed. San Antonio, Tex.: Historical Publishing Network, 2011. Print.

Mangus, Mike. '54Th Regiment Ohio Volunteer Infantry'. *Ohio Civil War Central.* N. p., 2011. Web. 3 Jun. 2014.

Marland, Faye and Harold. *The Epoch of the Park Street School, 1853-1964 and Grove City, Ohio.*

Martin, William T. *History Of Franklin County.* 1st ed. Columbus: Follett, Forster & Co., 1858. Print.

McNutt, Randy, and Cheryl Bauer. *Ohio Civil War Tales: A Primer of Copperheads, Hotheads, Tinclads, Abolitionists, Train Thieves, & Quantrill's Missing Skull.* 1st ed. Milford, Ohio: Little Miami Pub. Co., 2009. Print.

Mycivilwar.com. 'Camp Chase Prisoner of War Camp'. N. p., 2014. Web. 6 May. 2013.

Nichols, E.W.T. 'Ohio Civil War 150 | Collections & Exhibits | The Great American What Is It? Chased By Copper-Heads'. Ohiocivilwar150.org. N. p., 2013. Web. 6 May. 2013.

References

Nps.gov. '12Th Regiment, Virginia Cavalry, Confederate Troops – Search for Battle Units – The Civil War (U.S. National Park Service)'. N. p., 2013. Web. 18 Jul. 2013.

Ohio Civil War Central. 'Charles H. Cole'. N. p., 2013. Web. 2 Jul. 2013.

Ohio, Roster Commission. *Official Roster of the Soldiers of the State Of Ohio In The War Of The Rebellion, 1861-1866, Volume 5*. 1st ed. Werner Company, 1887. Print.

'Ohio Civil War 150 | Collections & Exhibits | The Copperhead Plan for Subjugating the South / F.B.'. *Ohiocivilwar150.org*. N. p., 2014. Web. 6 May. 2013.

Osborn, George C. 'A Confederate Prisoner at Camp Chase: Letters and A Diary of Private James W. Anderson'. *Ohio History*. N. p., 1998. Web. 28 Apr. 2013.

Pendleton, Nancy J. *Early Clintonville (and Grove City) and the Bull and Smith Families*. Columbus, OH. 1997.

Perkins, Marlitta. 'Camp Chase – Inspection Report, March 11, 1865'. N. p., 2005. Web. 2 Apr. 2014.

Religion in Ohio. 1st ed. Ohio Memory, 2012. Web. 1 Jul. 2013.

Rippley, LaVern. *The German-Americans*. 1st ed. Boston: Twayne publ., 1976. Print.

Shailer, Janet, and Laura Lanese. *Grove City*. 1st ed. Charleston, SC: Arcadia Pub., 2008. Print.

Smith & Swinney,. 'Ohio Civil War 150 | Collections & Exhibits | The Soldier's Song—Unionism Vs. Copperheadism'. *Ohiocivilwar150.org*. N. p., 2013. Web. 6 May. 2013.

Stern, Alfred Withal. 'Ohio Civil War 150 | Collections & Exhibits | Editorial Cartoon, "Slow & Steady Wins the Race" By Alfred Withal Stern'. *Ohiocivilwar150.org*. N. p., 2013. Web. 6 May. 2013.

Studer, Jacob Henry. *Columbus, Ohio: Its History, Resources, And Progress*. 1st ed. [Columbus, Ohio]: [J.H. Studer], 1873. Print.

Taylor, James D. 'Camp Chase Letters'. *Datasync.com/JTaylor*. N. p., 2001. Web. 20 May. 2014.

Taylor, William Alexander. *Centennial History of Columbus and Franklin County, Ohio*. 1st ed. Chicago: S.J. Clarke Pub. Co., 1909. Print.

The Ohio State Journal Daily. 1865 : n. pag. Print.

Touring-ohio.com. 'Camp Chase: Civil War Prisoner of War Camp and Cemetery'. N. p., 2013. Web. 26 Apr. 2013.

References

Wagner, Nancy. 'Civil War Camps in Columbus, OH. Travel Tips by Demand Media.'. *USA Today*. N. p., 2013. Web. 27 Apr. 2013.

Weisenburger, Francis P. *Columbus During the Civil War*. 1st ed. [Columbus]: Ohio State University Press for the Ohio Historical Society, 1963. Print.

Welker, Martin. *Farm Life in Central Ohio Sixty Years Ago*. 1st ed. [Cleveland]: N. p., 1895. Print.

Wikipedia. 'Congregational Church'. N. p., 2013. Web. 1 Jul. 2013.

Burbiek, William. "Columbus, Ohio, theater from the beginning of the Civil War to 1875." Electronic Thesis or Dissertation. Ohio State University, 1963. *OhioLINK Electronic Theses and Dissertations Center*. 15 Jul 2015.

Also Available

Books by Belinda Kroll
Haunting Miss Trentwood
Catching the Rose

Stories by Belinda Kroll
The Story of Mad Maxine

Books by Binaebi Akah
Beatrice Learns to Dance
Sketchnotes Field Guide for the
Busy Yet Inspired Professional

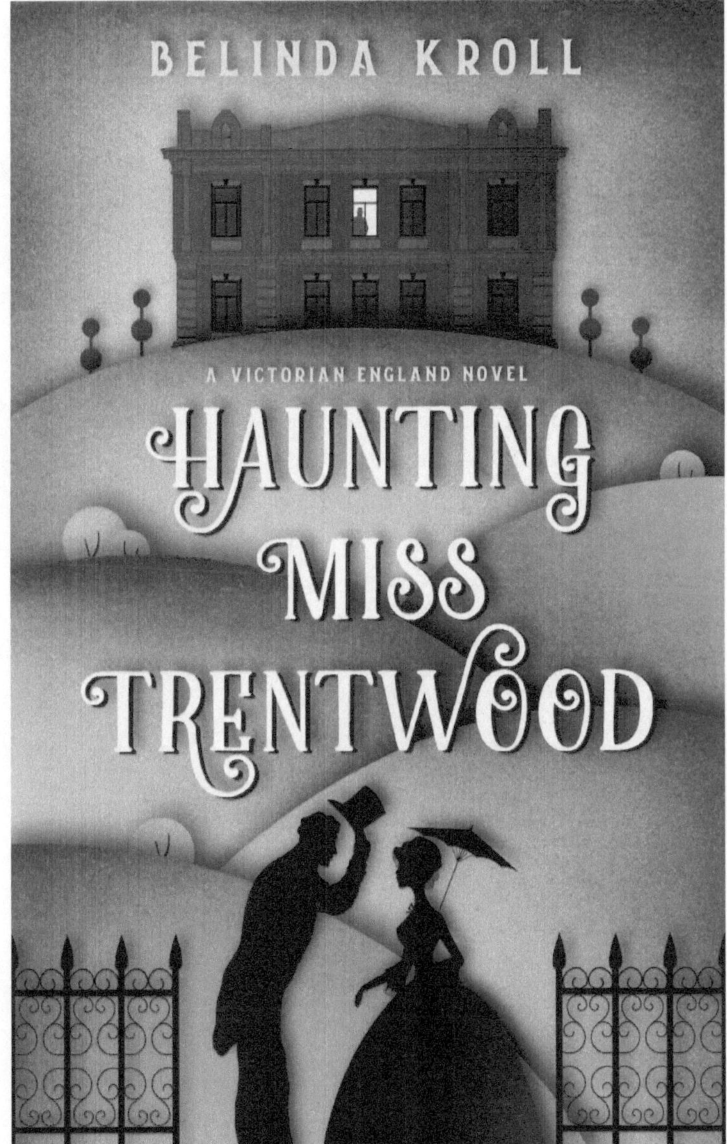

BELINDA KROLL
A VICTORIAN ENGLAND NOVEL
HAUNTING MISS TRENTWOOD

Witty, secluded Mary is adjusting to life with her aunt after her father, Trentwood, passes away and returns in ghostly form. Despite the urging of her spectral father, Mary continues to live in their aging home with only her aunt and their servants for company.

But their quiet manor house carries secrets even from Mary and Trentwood. When Hartwell, a London lawyer, arrives at their doorstep claiming someone in the house is blackmailing his sister, Mary stumbles into a mystery that forces her to revisit memories and rethink her future.

As Mary and Hartwell seek the blackmailer, each learns about the importance of opening one's heart to trust and betrayal. *Haunting Miss Trentwood* is a comedic gothic tale (think Legend of Sleepy Hollow meets Casper) written from varied perspectives. Readers will be entertained by bright dialogue and encouraged to reflect on the universal themes of dealing with parents and disappointing relationships, and learning to love again.

Excerpt from Haunting Miss Trentwood

Compton Beauchamp (three days ride west of London), February 1887

At two in the afternoon the coffin of Mary Trentwood's father was lowered to its grave. The sun shone unseasonably bright. Mary squinted through burning eyes. She heard the wooden box hit the bottom of the hole. She heard the whispers of her servants and father's friends behind her. However quietly they thought they were speaking, Mary heard every word. The whispers grew louder and moved closer, crowding her ears.

"Right barmy, that's what she is."

"I heard she hasn't any feeling at all."

"Certainly would explain the lack of tears."

"Making us stand here and watch the digging of the grave, it's indecent, that's what it is."

"Well, I certainly don't know how you can expect any better from hermits, they're not fit to be gentry, I say."

Mary didn't know who they were, these people whispering about her as she stood a mere four feet in front of them. She didn't care. They weren't there for her, they—whoever they were for she hadn't invited them, no, that had been the workings of her aunt Mrs. Durham—only cared about their gossip mongering. The local farmers and tenants would never treat her thus. But the funeral guests were certain to spread their hissing rumors across the countryside. Mary hated that unnamed mass of huddled, whispering heads standing behind her. She hated her father for dying, for making this entire ordeal necessary in the first place.

The vicar finished his sermon and snapped his Bible shut.

Mary hunched her shoulders as the mourners filed past. She gritted her teeth, but allowed the men to solemnly brush their lips against her gloved fingers. Her jaw all but shattered in her effort to not scream at the women making tut-tutting noises.

And then Mary was alone, her black netted veil scratching her pale cheek as the wind blew. She stared at that father-sized hole. She stepped closer. How close to the edge did she dare tread? How soon before her nerves, strained to their last, snapped, rendering her as lifeless as her dear father at the bottom of that dark pit?

Mary jumped when Mrs. Durham's hand touched her arm.

Mrs. Durham was a squat woman, with soft features that hinted at great beauty, once. Once upon a time, a very long time ago, Mary figured. Mrs. Durham had been her mother's twin, fraternally speaking. Mary was glad she didn't resemble her aunt in the slightest. Mrs. Durham's cheeks arched upward—reaching, straining, pushing—trying to touch the topmost curve of her eye sockets. Truly an appalling sight; Mary decided her aunt should never squint, if she could help it.

"Come away," Mrs. Durham murmured, "let the men folk do their job." She shifted so Mary's view of the gravediggers filling the grave was blocked. She began pushing Mary back to the manor house, where a light luncheon waited for them.

Whatever suggestive power Mrs. Durham had on Mary could not prevent the horrifying vision of a man, muddy and coughing, clawing his way from the grave site. He hung from the edge of the hole into which Trentwood's coffin had descended, his elbows digging into the dirt as he wriggled his way out.

Mary stared open-mouthed.

He was dismayingly flexible, able to swing a leg over the edge and roll onto the disturbed ground. He stood, brushing himself off almost apologetically though no dirt clung to his clothing. He gave Mary time to study his determined chin, firm mouth, and snappish eyes. He combed his sandy hair back from his forehead while clearing his throat, revealing streaks of gray running from temple to crown. The overall effect was chilling familiarity.

Mary wrenched free of Mrs. Durham. "Father?" she said, her voice hoarse from not speaking the week since his death. "Papa?"

~

Mary sat upright, kicking her bed sheets away from sweat-soaked legs. A lock of her dark hair was plastered to her cheek. Her head ached from the bobby pins still shoved into her scalp. She lifted her hand to pull the bobby pins out and noticed she was wearing black crepe sleeves, the same she wore in her nightmare.

Her hands shook. She hadn't been dreaming. Mary knew she hadn't been dreaming. She had buried her father, and he had crawled from his grave right before her eyes.

Her bedroom door opened to reveal Mrs. Durham with a tray of tea. "Oh good," Mrs. Durham said with false cheer, "you're finally awake."

"Finally?" Mary said. Her voice was no more than an awkward croak, but it seemed Mrs. Durham understood her.

"You've been sleeping for three days."

Mary shook her head. She gasped. Three days? Had it been three days since she had buried her father? Panting, she unbuttoned her dress to her collar bone, unable to inhale with the neck buttoned to her chin. She felt so hot. Why hadn't anyone undressed her? Right, that's right, she had dismissed her maid after her father died to alleviate costs.

Mary shook her head again as Mrs. Durham placed the tea tray on the little table beside her bed. Everything felt fuzzy.

Mrs. Durham sat in the vanity chair that had been dragged to the bedside while Mary slept. Her black dress rustled sweetly as she moved, the fabric shining in the gray sunlight. "You fainted dead away after the coffin went down."

Mary sighed. "Yes, I just—I thought I saw Papa."

"But you did, my dear."

Mary's hazel eyes narrowed to slits. "I did?"

"Well, do forgive my callousness, but I'm not certain who else you think we buried."

Mary felt a retort forming, but she held her tongue. She had to remember her aunt had lost her dear husband only four months ago, and was still out of sorts. She took the time to study Mrs. Durham shiny black earrings, the way her hands folded in her lap, the perfection of her graying hair pulled into a tight chignon topped with white lace.

Do I tell her? Do I admit I saw Father crawl from his grave? No, Mrs. Durham was not one for believing such "folderol" as she called it when Mary confided her nightmares or shared folklore and haunting stories with the servants.

Mary looked at the bedroom door, not hearing the raucous laughter of the funeral guests. "Where is everyone?" Mary asked instead, accepting a lukewarm cup of tea.

"Ah, I sent them home. Well," Mrs. Durham chuckled, "they left fairly quickly on their own. They were quite startled when you announced you wanted everyone to follow the coffin to its grave. What in the world made you do such a thing? It simply isn't done."

No, it wasn't done, but then, there were a great many things that Mary had done to satisfy Society, and she had decided that Society, in turn, could grant her this one aberration. Mary swallowed the last of the tea and placed the cup on the tray. "I'm rather tired."

Mrs. Durham frowned, hearing the finality in Mary's tone. "Of course," she replied, standing. "I trust you will send for me should you need me?" At Mary's silent nod, she took her leave, looking none too pleased.

As soon as the door was shut, Mary threw her hands to her face. "I did not see my father's ghost." She shivered despite being drenched with sweat. "I must be mad."

"A bit dramatic, I suppose, but mad? Would I allow you to run my household if you were mad?"

Mary screamed. She grabbed her skirts and scrambled atop her headboard.

At the foot of her bed stood her father. At least, she thought it was her father. It certainly looked just like him. Trentwood stood as he always had when lecturing her, hands clasped behind his back with a stern look on his face. "So you didn't see me, eh?"

About the Author

Belinda Kroll is the author of three historical novels, as well as non-fiction and children's storybooks under another name. Kroll grew up in a home where reading was encouraged and *Jeopardy!* was on every weeknight. Both activities fostered her love of history. She lives with her husband and two dogs in Ohio.

Read more at worderella.com / belindakroll.com.